PUFFIN CANADA

BEYOND BLONDE

TERESA TOTEN is the author of *Better Than Blonde* and three other young adult novels, including *The Game* and *Me and the Blondes,* which were both shortlisted for the Governor General's Award. Her most recent book is *Piece by Piece: Stories About Fitting into Canada.*

www.teresatoten.com

Also by Teresa Toten

Piece by Piece: Stories About Fitting into Canada

Better Than Blonde

Me and the Blondes

Onlyhouse

The Game

Bright Red Kisses
(a picture book)

You are so Beyond Beautiful

Beyond Blonde

love

Teresa Toten

PUFFIN
CANADA

PUFFIN CANADA

Published by the Penguin Group

Penguin Group (Canada), 90 Eglinton Avenue East, Suite 700,
Toronto, Ontario, Canada M4P 2Y3 (a division of Pearson Canada Inc.)

Penguin Group (USA) Inc., 375 Hudson Street, New York, New York 10014, U.S.A.
Penguin Books Ltd, 80 Strand, London WC2R 0RL, England
Penguin Ireland, 25 St Stephen's Green, Dublin 2, Ireland (a division of Penguin Books Ltd)
Penguin Group (Australia), 250 Camberwell Road, Camberwell, Victoria 3124, Australia
  (a division of Pearson Australia Group Pty Ltd)
Penguin Books India Pvt Ltd, 11 Community Centre, Panchsheel Park,
  New Delhi – 110 017, India
Penguin Group (NZ), 67 Apollo Drive, Rosedale, North Shore 0745, Auckland, New Zealand
  (a division of Pearson New Zealand Ltd)
Penguin Books (South Africa) (Pty) Ltd, 24 Sturdee Avenue, Rosebank, Johannesburg 2196,
  South Africa

Penguin Books Ltd, Registered Offices: 80 Strand, London WC2R 0RL, England

First published 2010

1 2 3 4 5 6 7 8 9 10 (WEB)

Copyright © Teresa Toten, 2010

Manufactured in Canada.

LIBRARY AND ARCHIVES CANADA CATALOGUING IN PUBLICATION

Toten, Teresa, 1955–
  Beyond blonde / Teresa Toten.

ISBN 978-0-14-317358-8

I. Title.

PS8589.O6759B49 2011   jC813'.54   C2010-905853-4

Visit the Penguin Group (Canada) website at **www.penguin.ca**

Special and corporate bulk purchase rates available; please see
www.penguin.ca/corporatesales or call 1-800-810-3104, ext. 2477 or 2474

In memory of Janja Vukovic
Mama

Always tell the truth. Even if you have to make it up.

—*AUTHOR UNKNOWN*

Beyond Blonde

Prologue

Mama turns on the water in the bathtub, hoping it will drown out her crying. It never does. The condo walls are paper-thin, practically see-through.

My Euclid Avenue bedroom had gorgeous thick walls, but that was before prison. The condo is after. The Euclid room was awesome. I think. I *know* that the walls were awesome because Papa and I painted them electric orange one Sunday while he was in that sweet spot between four and seven shots of brandy. I can't really nail down any of the other details. My orange room blurs into the five other bedrooms I've had since we've moved from there to here.

My condo bedroom is beige, bar none the most pathetic colour in the known universe. We've been here for almost three years, Mama, me, and, for a minute and a half, Papa, and it's like my bedroom is still in its underwear. I plopped onto my mattress, which is on the floor, and stared at it all accusingly. At least I had this brilliant lava lamp that Auntie Eva gave me when I turned sixteen. The lamp's bobbing purple blobs float on top of a stack of *Encyclopaedia Britannica*s, A through P. We couldn't afford the rest, or the Britannica people couldn't keep up with our moves. I forget which. Given the room, the lamp looked like it was trying way too hard.

I knew how it felt.

I also had Papa's mirror, the one he made me for my eighth birthday on Euclid Avenue. It had the best bits of my little-girl self glued, shellacked, and frozen onto its frame. I had a home then. I haven't called any of the places "home" since then. But that was *then*. Now, Papa's gone again, and Mama's relapsed right back into her Papa in Prison behaviour. She's either all over me or spending entire weekends in her room, crying as quietly as she can. She just hit hour three of smothered sobbing. I lay down. Jesus God even the ceiling was beige! I never noticed that before. Isn't there some kind of decorating law that ceilings have to be white?

He'll come back when he's sober. He said. He packed up his shirts, his poetry books, some of my art, and all of his laughter. Papa packed up his making me feel like his princess, and he left.

His drinking, his leaving, their "separation," her crying— none of it was my fault. I know that. I've seen all the Afterschool Specials. But there must have been at least some little thing that I could have, should have, done but did not do. My head is swirling with free-floating crappy bits.

I need something. I need a thing to help fill up the hole inside me, or at least to muffle the echo a bit, not a booze thing or a dope thing, or even a guy thing … but a *some* thing. For sure, I need a *something*.

On the bright side, I don't have any secrets left.

Unless you count the ones you keep from yourself.

The Blondes still have enough secrets to sink a ship. Sure, Madison came clean about her adoption, but she's still passing off her loony grandma as a former housekeeper. Sarah insists that she's a born-again virgin, but she's straining under the weight of all that purity. And then there's Kit, who swore seven ways from Sunday that she's done with the puking. Kit's got a therapist and a plan, and she says that she's sticking to both. Maybe, but I can smell a secret from a thousand paces, and you can bottle the scent coming off her.

Not off me though. Like I said, I am secretless.

I am now the holder of *their* secrets, but they are not *my* secrets. Papa in prison was a secret, a big one. Luke and I were a secret, almost as big, maybe bigger. No more. My first love was, as of last February, officially married *and* a brand-new daddy. So, we're dead, done, finished, over. When I lie now, it's for the Blondes, not for me. That kind of lying doesn't even count as lying. It's more like community service.

Still, listening to Mama scares me. I mean, what if that's as good as it gets for her? Even worse … what if this is as good as it gets for me? What if good things just don't happen to people like us? It's possible, given us being immigrants and given prison, the drinking, the moves, my life so far. And then I think, *no.…* No way.

I exhale, get up, and shut the door on Mama.

It works.

There's no more crying.

We were about as inconspicuous as a three-ring circus in a monastery.

"Don't pushing!"

"Who vas pushing?"

"You vas pushing!"

"I vas never no how pushing!"

"Shhht, shhht!"

Mama of all people should have known better. The Aunties were unshakably unshushable. Yes, they adored her, and maybe they were even a little afraid of her, but *nobody* shushes the Aunties. It didn't matter that they had, hand to heart, agreed to Mama's game plan in the parking lot a cool three minutes ago. "Vatever happens …" Mama made eye contact with each one of them. "Vonce ve are in da Anonymous Alcohol meeting …" They nodded with an enthusiasm that made their beehive hairdos lurch. "Ve must to be totally, completely, inconspicuous, *da*?"

"*Pa,* sure!" harrumphed Auntie Eva.

"Tootally incognito," agreed Auntie Radmila.

"Everybodies vill tink ve are drunks!" promised Auntie Luba.

Mama winced. "Just remember: *inconspicuous.*" Heartfelt nodding all around.

Not a chance.

For one thing, we had just not so inconspicuously exited Luigi's White Night limousine, a gleaming white super stretch that was tricked out in twinkle lights. You could see that thing from the moon. Luigi was still trying to manoeuvre it out of the parking lot as we clambered down the steps to the church basement. Luigi Pescatore was Auntie Eva's latest and most enthusiastic beau. They met last year when we used his limo service for Auntie Luba's monster wedding to Mike. The moment that Luigi set eyes on Auntie Eva in her one-of-a-kind "kinda couture" bridesmaid's dress, he was gunning to be husband number five. As of last Friday, Auntie Eva had rather grudgingly agreed to put him out of his misery. It was a slick compromise. They were officially unofficially engaged. Jewellery was involved, but the date was murky.

The other not-so-inconspicuous thing is that we arrived in a clump. All the other alcoholics were filing in by themselves or, on occasion, meeting someone outside and then coming in. Auntie Eva picked an AA meeting in Rosedale because she insisted that we'd get a better class of drunk here. And, so far, she was right. All the alcoholics were pressed, groomed, or, at the very least, clean.

Still, none of them looked like they were going to the El Mocambo circa 1962, which was standard Auntie streetwear. Mama was the muted one in a bright Pepto-Bismol pink "almost Chanel" suit that she saved for closing real estate deals. The Aunties never went anywhere without full armour: hair teased and sprayed, makeup blazing, girdles girdling, and billowing silk outfits meant to dazzle, if not blind, all potential opponents.

Mama made me iron my jeans. Shuffling around with pressed bell-bottoms only added to my escalating anxiety about being here in the first place. I had this vague but persistent feeling that AA was a seriously secret society. What if they could tell I was an impostor? They probably had a deeply humiliating throw-the-fraud-out ritual that involved strobe lights and sirens. I felt terrible that I didn't have a drinking problem. Auntie Eva assured us that even "sober peoples vas velcome to za Open Meetings," but given the source, I didn't believe it for a minute.

Just going down the steps felt like lying … something you'd think I'd be comfortable with by now.

As soon as we got to the bottom of the stairs, we were put through a greeting gauntlet.

"Welcome, man."

A very tall gentleman wearing granny glasses and an eye-popping swirly T-shirt smiled sweetly at us. "Peace, eh, and have a cool meeting." His head was covered in a thousand tiny moving braids. The guy was a walking willow tree. Auntie

Eva ignored his outstretched hand and fingered his T-shirt instead.

"Darrrling, zis is too fantastik. How did you do zis?"

Dear Lord.

"Sophie, psst, Sophie!" Auntie Radmila grabbed my ear. "Iz zis a homosexual-type person?"

"No, Auntie Radmila," I whispered as I bent down. "He's a hippie."

"Ah! A hippie!" she beamed at him. *"Pa da!" Pa da* means "of course" in Croatian. The exclamation mark is implied.

We disengaged Auntie Eva from the hippie's shirt and were promptly accosted by a tidy, middle-aged man in a dove-grey suit. Then there was an imposing Native in a suede, fringed jacket. He was followed by a nice librarian-type lady. "Welcome," she said as she shook our hands with both of hers. Somewhere in all that handshaking, I stopped being afraid of being a fraud. We shook hands with thousands of people. Each of them made eye contact, grabbed our hands, smiled, and welcomed us in. Welcomed? It was like walking into a hug. Powerful stuff.

A little old lady who was shaped like a comma and wearing a blue tracksuit pointed with her cigarette to some empty seats near the podium. Wow, there had to be a couple of hundred chairs put out. How many drunks did they have in Rosedale? "There's still five seats together on the left side," she rasped. "It's a great spot for you kids."

Mama hugged her.

Shoot me dead.

Auntie Eva wished her luck with her "sobering."

"Sobriety," I corrected as we marched *inconspicuously* up to the front.

"*Zat* is vat I said," she sniffed.

An impressive fog hovered just above our heads. Pretty much everyone in the place was smoking like a coal furnace and mainlining coffee. As we made our way up to the third row, random people smiled at us between puffs and sips. It could have been creepy in a saffron, Hare-Krishna kind of way. Instead, I never wanted to leave. I wanted to stay here with these people, these nice men and women who appeared to be so delighted that I had come. It was like they didn't care what I did or didn't do before I got here; they were just happy I was there.

Was this how it felt for Papa? Especially after all those years spent in prison for something he didn't do but was too damn drunk to know he didn't do? Maybe that stuff wouldn't matter here.

Behind the podium, giant rolling blackboards with beautifully scripted sayings reminded us that *There, but for the Grace of God* and *You are no longer alone.*

I looked around. Just about every seat was taken. Hand-lettered posters taped to the institutional-green basement walls bore witness to the Twelve Steps you always hear about.

1. We admitted we were powerless over alcohol—that our lives had become unmanageable.

Powerless—I got that part. I've been feeling pretty powerless myself. Auntie Eva and I read the rest of them. God was in most of the steps and on all of the posters. In fact, God was all over the place. We were in a church basement, after all. I kept looking around. Even some of the more agitated guys looked like they had a chance at *calm*. Were they all believers? Did they switch out booze for God? The room was filling up fast. No doubt about it, the drunks looked normal, better than normal even. Maybe there was something to the God thing. I wondered how that went down with Papa who was a card-carrying non-believer. Papa's aggressive atheism was one of the thousand things that made Auntie Eva mental. Still, to every-one's astonishment, she let Papa stay in her basement apartment when he left us last February to find himself and sobriety.

Apparently, Papa went to an AA meeting at least three times a week, and there were weeks when he went every single night. Auntie Eva said that she was going to burst a kidney unless she got to see what they did here. That was no doubt true, but I think she mainly wanted to give Mama a boost. Mama was wobbly again. What no one gets, except me and the Aunties, is that Mama is even more of a tortured, poetic soul than Papa. It's just that she wraps it in so much hyper-achievement and noise that she confuses people.

Auntie Eva told me that this meeting would show Mama how "za light alveys goes out in za tunnel." Yeah. I just let those go. If you think too hard about any "Auntie sayings," you get a little nauseated.

What *I* wanted was Papa home, drunk or sober. Yesterday.

7. Humbly asked Him to remove our shortcomings.

I liked that one. Make someone else responsible for my

shortcomings! Or at the very least, get God to do the heavy lifting. Yeah. I could get the AA God to "remove" my addiction to Luke Pearson. Even though we were so obviously over, I still dreamed about Luke every single night and could still smell the Sunlight Soap of him at any given moment.

A man sporting a puff of white hair and a blue knit sweater bounded up to the podium. "Good evening, and welcome." He smiled. "My named is Peter and I'm an alcoholic."

We, each of us, gasped. I mean to just come out and say it like that, out loud, and in front of people!

Everybody else said, "Hi Peter."

"As always, we'll start with a moment of silence and then the Serenity Prayer."

Everyone stood up.

In our panic to blend in, we jumped up with a bit too much enthusiasm. Auntie Luba and Mama overturned their chairs. Inconspicuous? It felt like the rest of the room was bathed in darkness except for the klieg light aimed at our row. Auntie Eva squealed when an accountant type beside her grabbed her hand. Apparently, you hold hands to pray here.

"God grant me the serenity ..."

Everybody else knew the words.

"To accept the things I cannot change."

Well this was awkward.

"Courage to change the things I can."

Still, there was such a powerful feeling in the room, warmth and what—safety? Is that what you feel, Papa? Do you feel safe here?

"And the wisdom to know the difference."

And that was it, the whole prayer. We sat down again. Next time I was going to bring a pen so I could write things down. Next time?

There were four more speakers.

"Hi, my name is Steven and I'm an alcoholic."

"Hi Steven."

"Hi, my name is Doris and I'm an alcoholic."

We came in with everyone on the "Hi Doris" and felt very proud of ourselves.

"Hi, my name is John and I'm an alcoholic."

"Hi John."

We were old pros by John.

John reminded us how important the anonymous part was. "Everything in this room stays in this room. We must never acknowledge each other on the outside." John also spoke in honour of his friend Bob, who was getting something called a one-year medallion. But first John gave us a taste of his own life before AA, which involved the loss of his family and many, many hospitalizations. But now he'd been sober for twelve years and could be of service to people like Bob, who'd apparently been sober, one day at a time, from September 1975 to today, September 3, 1976. Someone should make a movie about this stuff. Bob got up.

"Hi, my name is Bob and I'm an alcoholic."

"Hi Bob."

Bob told us about his descent into the bottle after his daughter was killed by a drunk driver. He talked about his guilt and shame, his addictions to both pain pills and alcohol. He told us about losing jobs, humiliating his family, and going through years of multiple benders and blackouts. I had a cringing flashback of me and Madison combing the city, bar by bar, searching for Papa. Bob talked about all of this without once sounding like he felt sorry for himself. He talked about Jesus Christ, his personal saviour, and his sponsor-saviour, John. Finally, in a rough whisper, Bob talked about the steadfast love of his wife, Judy. Auntie Luba and Auntie Eva were sobbing by the time he was actually presented with his medallion to honour 365 days of sobriety.

After the applause died down, Peter, our host for the evening, returned to the podium. The air charged and tensed, the smoke dispersed into different patterns. Peter stared at us for a good long time. What was he looking for? Finally, he exhaled. "It begins here, people. Does anyone have nine months of sobriety?"

Silence. You could hear us all breathing, but there were no takers.

"Six months?"

Our Native greeter in the fringed coat and a middle-aged man in a short-sleeved plaid shirt bounded up to receive a small red token and a very enthusiastic round of applause.

"Three months?"

A guy in chinos and a button-down shirt strode up like he was going to receive an Oscar. He got even louder applause. It was like the shorter you were sober, the louder was your applause.

"One month?"

A pause, tension built, and then three people from different parts of the room leapt up and made their way to the podium.

Wild applause for two older men and a lady in a faded tracksuit! Wow, she looked like everybody's grandmother and she had been sober just a month? This place was amazing.

"Now …" Peter scanned through the smoke into the room. None of us breathed. "Is there anybody in this room who can commit to 24 hours of sobriety? Just 24 hours?"

A skinny young guy in blue jeans and a red T-shirt with a big black peace symbol on the front jumped up. And so did— oh Jesus God no—the kerfuffle in our aisle was unmistakable.

Shoot me dead and make it quick.

Auntie Eva was making her way to the podium.

I turned and glared at Mama.

"Vat could I do?" she shrugged. "She vas carrying avay by da moments." Auntie Radmila, who had held it together up until now, wept profusely.

"Auntie Radmila! Stop that. She isn't even …" What could I say? She knew as well as I did that Auntie Eva liked her brandy, as did all of the Aunties, but she was no more an alcoholic than I was, and I didn't drink. It felt like the room and God himself erupted into an explosion of applause. Auntie Eva hugged the skinny kid, her 24-hour-commitment partner, and the applause went nuclear. Our little area kept clapping until she sat down and shamelessly showed off her little white token to our seatmates, who mouthed "bravo" and "we're here for you" while she pretended to blush.

Peter reminded us all that, no matter how cruel or unwelcoming the world was outside, inside we were welcome and safe, one day at a time. The meeting was over. People streamed by us, eager to encourage Auntie Eva, shaking her hand, touching her shoulder. I glared at her. No good, she didn't notice. She was still bathing in her commitment, her triumph, her applause. I could see why Papa came over and over again.

It was addictive.

Okay. Made it. Cross it off the list. I survived yet another first day of school! Given my pitiful history of multiple schools and multiple humiliations, I say that with genuine surprise and relief. Today was also the first day of grade eleven, the first day of senior basketball practice, the first day of me and the Blondes getting together after a summer of being blown about, and the first day back to having lunch together at Mike's. And all those firsts had gone about as good as they could go.

So why was I so twitchy back at the condo?

I dropped my books on the floor and glared at the living room like it was to blame. No. Our place was smallish, okay teeny, but it was way cool and it *was* ours. The Blondes all lived in spectacular *Architectural Digest* places, but even they had never seen anything like our condo. Condos were still a pretty weird concept, owning an apartment basically, but Mama swore that they would take off. That's what she does when she isn't locked in her room or riding me about my grades: she's a real estate agent. Now, the last of the lazy afternoon sun slipped in from the floor-to-ceiling windows in the living room. That wall of windows overlooking Toronto's treetops always made it seem like the condo was showing off.

I loved that.

I tiptoed over to the closed bedroom door and knocked.

"Mama?"

Nothing. I opened the door. No one. She was either at the office or showing condos to nervous Anglicans. At least she wasn't entombed in here. Instead of shutting the door or going in, I hovered in the doorway. I've been hovering a lot lately.

Mama repainted her bedroom in Benjamin Moore's Smouldering Red the minute she knew Papa was getting out of prison. I took a step in. It was like walking into a bottle of wine. I stopped and leaned back against the door. All traces of Papa were erased. No lingering smell of smoke, no swaggering "male" scent. There wasn't a single tie or stray sock behind that closed closet door. I knew this from a thousand other inspections. The bench at the foot of the bed that once held his beaten-up tobacco-coloured suitcase was aggressively empty.

Gone.

Mama's perfume bottle collection sat on the windowsill, waiting for me. It was her only indulgence. I loved them as much as she did. The bottles caught and held the light, making it dance against the deep burgundy walls. Each one captured a promise of fairy dust and dreams, but the bottle that held the most magic was the *L'Air du Temps* with its entwined crystal swallows. I could never resist touching it, stroking those beautiful birds, making a wish.

Wishes that came, but didn't stay, true. This time, I put the bottle back and walked out of the room without making a wish. That was kid stuff.

I shut the door.

I could turn into her. Jesus God what a thought. I could turn into my mother … a flame-throwing drama queen who was never satisfied with anything or anyone. A diva who drives her husband to drink, drives him away, and then gets depressed because he's gone! Auntie Eva says that I couldn't turn into Mama because I'm not sensitive enough to get depressed. Okay, she means well, but I hate the "not sensitive enough" part. I'm plenty sensitive. Still, even now with Papa gone, I couldn't work up into a decent depression. I was just a bunch of *A* words. I looked them up when I was searching for various definitions of *addiction* and *alcoholic*. At this very moment, I believe I am suffering from being *annoyed, anxious, adolescent, agonized, anguished, ambivalent, angry, apathetic, ashamed,* and *anemic*. Well, maybe not anemic. I just liked the way it sounds and the pictures it conjured up. You just know that an anemic-type person is going to be very sensitive.

I grabbed a Coke and went into the safety of my own room. Mistake. I got *annoyed* all over again. All my clothes were folded into razor-sharp neat little piles on the floor.

A crazy person lived here.

Mama said that I could do up my room any way I wanted. I just couldn't get my head around it somehow. I've read magazine articles about this. Rooms say stuff about you. Like Mama's red room and her lying perfume bottles.

Kit's bedroom was all space age and modern. She had a shag rug that we kept losing stuff in and furniture that was tubular and plastic, sorry, laminate and lacquer, that was painted in lime greens and mellow yellows. Kit's room was fun and bold, with a touch of freezer burn. I rest my case.

Sarah's bedroom was swathed in matching lilac and mint-green flowers. There were lilacs on her curtains, on her overstuffed pillows, and all over her linens. Her furniture was either cream or princess white, including a little girl's canopy bed that she couldn't part with.

Madison's room, her suite really, was almost as big as our apartment. All the fabrics were juicy yellows and blues, but the furniture was way weird. Every stick of it was old; they were antiques passed down from generation to generation. None of it matched. When you're that rich, you can't have things match. Matching was for poor people. I think all that old stuff soothed her adopted soul.

I took in the "I haven't moved in yet" quality of my room. *Oy.*

At least I had my mirror.

I examined the upper-left-hand corner. It got chipped in the last move. Right below the chip and tucked under a Mr. Potato Head was a crystal rosary that I hadn't noticed before. The mirror did that, showed me new things and hid old ones. I touched the rosary and automatically made the sign of the cross. That felt good. Maybe I was a closet Catholic. Okay, maybe not, but I remembered that there

was a ton of God at the AA meeting. I also remembered
that all that God stuff seemed to settle down a room full
of anxious alcoholics. Come to think of it, it settled me
down too. Maybe I needed some holy help. Maybe that was
my *something*. Maybe God could chase away Luke. I was
fumbling around in my limited database of religions when
the door blew open. Mama was instantly behind me, staring
at me, at us, in my mirror.

"Mama!" I groaned. "I've been telling you for three years
to knock!"

"I know you said …" Mama wrapped her arms around me.
"Sorry, sorry." She kissed the back of my head. "How vas our
first day of school? I been tinking about you non-stopping."

"*My* first day was fine." She didn't let go, just waited for
more.

Much to my irritation, I delivered.

"Mr. Wymeran, our senior girls' basketball coach, has
called in the Mounties after our disastrous season last year."

Mama nodded, pretending to understand the Mountie
reference.

"So, he's bringing in David Walter, the captain of the senior
boys' team, to assist for the whole season. The boys have been
city champions for two years in a row, and David was captain
for both years."

"Good?" she asked.

"Yeah, sure." I shrugged. "We need the help. We're still
young for a senior team." Mama smiled. I could tell she
thought this was a good thing rather than the liability it was.
Despite the fact that she hunted down every game I'd ever

played in, Mama still didn't understand the first thing about basketball. Basketball was Papa's game.

"So, dis boy coach is very good ting, *da*?"

"*Da*, yeah, sure, maybe, don't know," I said. David used to be Luke's best friend. He was also beyond gorgeous. The whole team went on high alert as soon as he walked into the gym. Thing is, maybe he knew about Luke and me last year, even though we were a secret, and maybe he felt sorry for Alison, I mean, the new Mrs. Luke Pearson. Okay, none of that made sense, but I just couldn't shake the feeling that David Walter got a rash when he looked at me.

"It's a wait-and-see kind of thing," I said.

"*Que sera, sera,* vatever vill be, vill be." Hand Mama a slice of uncertainty, and she'll hand you back a twenty-year-old Doris Day song.

"Uh, yeah." I wriggled out of her arm lock. "Have you talked to Papa this week?"

She nodded absently, taking in my clothes sculptures out of the corner of her eye. She sighed but swallowed anything she was going to offer up about the unfinished state of my room.

I was impressed. Good control on her part.

"It's not so crazy dis time, Sophie. Not like da last time, da prison time. Dis time vile he is away is totally positive, totally healty, and very good."

That was more like it. "Wow, you must not have been here for those weekends in the summer when you spent the whole time locked up in your room with a box of Kleenex."

"I don't like it ven you use da ironing tone vit me, Sophie," she sniffed.

"Ironic," I said. "And you mean sarcastic, not ironic."

"I *mean,* don't use dat voice to me." She patted her hair. "Dis is good. Papa vill drying out like a prune. Ve saw how it goes at da alcoholics' club." More hair patting. "Den he vill come home and stay to da home, finish."

Mama, who would rather undergo surgery with a stick than talk about any of this, walked over to my closet and pulled out a rolled-up poster. "Ve bought you dis poster two years ago, Sophie." She waved it at me accusingly. "Vhy don't you put it on your valls?"

My *Endless Summer* poster. I loved that thing. It was a heat source of burning oranges, flaming yellows, and hot pinks with a silhouette of a guy carrying a surfboard on his head. I've barely been on a ferry on Lake Ontario, but that poster made me believe I could surf monster waves on the Pacific. My room was not worthy of my poster. "Yeah, soon, Mama," I lied.

"Good." She smiled. I smiled back. It was our version of a truce, times when we pretended to believe each other rather than duke it out. Mama headed for the door and then turned her head. "Ven is your first big practice?"

"First full practice is tomorrow." Wait a minute. Mama might turn up. I hated it when she came to the games, let alone the practices. She was beyond embarrassing.

She reached for the door.

"Don't come, Mama."

I felt like a piece of gum as soon as the words were out of my mouth. I saw her shoulders tense through the suit-jacket fabric. "It's just a practice, after all. I'll bring you the game schedule as soon as I get it." Her shoulders lowered an inch as she reached for the handle.

"I vas being very busy anyvay," she said to the door. "You vill be captain?"

Good question. I was the best player. We both knew this. I was captain of the last two teams, when we were city champions as juniors and when we were blown out of the water last year, when me and the Blondes were made to move up too early into seniors. The Blondes would make sure that the team, whoever made the final cut, would vote for me, but someone like David would have a say, maybe a big say.

"Could be, maybe. I don't know. I don't want to talk about it."

"Sorry," she whispered to the door and left.

What was the matter with me? Thank God Mama signed a blood oath when I was born that she had to love me no matter what an awful twerp I was.

If only I had signed one too.

I had to admit we sucked. Okay, not as much as we sucked last year, but we were pretty slurpy all right. Mr. Wymeran put us through some basic drills for over an hour while David wrote things down on a clipboard. I hate that, clipboard writing I mean.

Our starting lineup was too young given that me and the Blondes were still in grade eleven, and Jessica Sherman, our probable left forward, was only in grade twelve. The other Toronto teams were more reasonably populated with kids that were a couple of years older than us. Ontario was the only place on the planet that had thirteen rather than twelve high school grades, and we had to be the only team in the province without a single grade thirteen player. The inevitable consequence of this was that every other team in the city was taller, heavier, and meaner than we were. This we knew from last year.

I kept telling myself that we now had a year of senior play under our tunics. We too were smarter, tougher, and then I looked at Kit, all sinew and gristle. Kit swore up and down that she hadn't barfed in a year, but our left guard still looked about as menacing as a pen stroke. Madison was our lone Amazon, clocking in at almost six feet, but she was willowy and graceful. She'd strike fear only into her fellow butterflies as she floated down the court. Sarah, dear God, was all breasts. Her practice jersey was strained to the breaking point, which made her a threat to the male coaches, but that was about it. Then there was me, 110 pounds of terror and five-foot-four, most of which was hair.

I didn't like our chances this year either.

Apparently neither did Mr. Wymeran, hence David's brooding presence.

There were sixteen of us on the senior team, first string, second string, and two alternates who also served as managers. The tryouts for the openings were held in the last week of August. For a fancy-pants school, Northern took its basketball shockingly seriously. Last year's first string, us, got a pass. Me and the Blondes were in no matter what, so we were scattered until Labour Day weekend. Madison came back from somewhere called the Lake District in England. Kit returned from spending the summer at her mother's place in Berkeley, California. And, although Sarah stayed around, she'd been consumed by the birth of a brand-new baby sister, the fifth blonde, blue-eyed girl in the Davis family collection. I spent the summer working at Mike's restaurant and milling around the city. I don't know about the Blondes, but I was incoherent with boredom and couldn't wait to get back to being "us."

Mr. Wymeran blew his whistle and called us over. "Not bad, ladies, not bad, but we're going to need a little more from you this year, right?" Most of us nodded. "So as you know, I got the team an extra pair of hands." He looked mighty pleased with himself. "David Walter will, as of today, be named assistant coach to our senior girls' team. His word is law, ladies." David stepped forward and flashed a smile at the left side of the room. There were audible sighs. I was on the *right* side of the room.

"Just in case anyone here doesn't know, David is the captain of our championship Northern Wildcats." Yeah well, I'd just been voted captain back in the dressing room. So here we were facing off captain to captain. His jaw clenched and unclenched. I felt a compulsion to touch it. "David has a lot of fine moves and skills to show us." This was greeted with very poorly suppressed giggles.

David winked at the girls on the *left* side. "Ladies." The entire second string sucked in their stomachs and played with their hair. Pathetic. I flashed to David and Luke horsing around at the third-floor lockers, coming into the restaurant with the football team on Saturday mornings, catching bits and pieces of our games over the past couple of years. He glanced at me gimlet-eyed before gracing the second string with another smile.

Or maybe it was all in my imagination.

"What the hell, buttercup?" Kit nudged me with her elbow. "Did you shoot his puppy or something?"

Or maybe not.

"Practices," David said, "will be at least two hours long. That's how we build a championship team."

"It'll take more than that." What the hell? Was that me? Yup, ready, shoot, aim, that's all you need to know about me.

"Yeah, Kan-din-sky." David drew out my name like he was trying to remember all of its component pieces. It took him an hour and a half to get to the -*sky* part. He looked me up and down and down and up, and I did the same: dark hair, black eyes, black lashes, and creamy skin. Actually, he was kind of a taller, maler, version of me … except, I swear, he was prettier. "But that's where we start, and *if* someone wants to be captain …"

If? *If!* Hey, I had just been voted captain. I *was* captain. What the hell, *if*?!

"Then maybe that potential captain should hold back on gratuitous comments and just be prepared to display some leadership skills." Everybody, including Mr. Wymeran, stared at the two of us staring at each other. Lines were being drawn in quicksand.

"Okay, ladies," huge hypnotic smile, "two miles with a drop twenty on every whistle."

The moaning crested into a rolling wave. Not me. I didn't even pause to exhale before I hit the track. I was joined by my team's not-so-graceful thumping on the boards, accompanied by a din of low-level muttering. Kit sped up to pass me. "Holy cowpie, he's definitely got a hard-on for you. What did you—"

"Oh, I agree," heaved Sarah behind us. "He's got a thing

for our Sophie." Kit and I rolled our eyes. Sarah was adorable but dumber than a bag of hair when it came to stuff like this.

Every time Mr. Wymeran called out an encouraging "just seventeen more laps to go" or something, David topped it up with a "pick up the pace, ladies," and then he'd whistle for a drop. My lungs were erupting by the third set of drops, and it felt like I was hauling a load of concrete instead of my legs, but I refused to sweat, let alone moan. I was not going to give the assistant coach that satisfaction. No way, no how, no—

"Yoohoo, sorry."

Oh … my … God … no.

"Yoohoo, yoohoo!"

I told her not to come. I was even mean about it. I clearly remember feeling guilty about the mean part!

"Sorry, yoohoo, everybodies!"

We all looked up. Mr. Wymeran looked up. David looked up. I refused to look up.

"Yoohoo, Sophia …"

I looked up. I could no longer pretend that I didn't know who that woman was. There she was hanging over the railings in the spectators' gallery that overlooked us. She was in danger of doing a half gainer onto the court. I broke out of the circle and ran over.

"Mama?!"

David was at my side in a flash. "Can I help you, uh, Mrs. Kandinsky? I'm David Walter, the—"

"Oooo, za new coach and so good looking and so tall and for sure, so good looking. Sophie said so."

If I got my hands on a basketball, I could pick her off and knock her unconscious....

"Sophie!" She grabbed a hanky out of her purse and dabbed at her dry eyes. "Iz a tragedy!" She clutched her chest. The whole team clutched their chests, including the Blondes, who really honestly, for sure, should have known better.

She was that good. Mama could turn picking up some milk into an opera.

"What is it, Mrs. Kandinsky?" Madison was already collecting her gear.

"Iz Uncle Luigi." More dabbing.

Uncle Luigi? Since when did Luigi become *Uncle* Luigi?

"He is dropping dead, may he rest in pieces." She made the sign of the cross. "Life is not a cabaret, old chum. Auntie Eva is behind herself. She is crazy vit good grief!"

David understandably looked confused. The Blondes, meanwhile, packed up their gear and mine in a nanosecond.

"Ve must to go." Sigh.

"Coming Mrs. K," called Kit.

"But ..." said David.

"Well, perhaps ..." said Mr. Wymeran.

"We'll meet you at the Pink Panther, Mrs. Kandinsky," called Madison. The Pink Panther was the pink Buick that Mama won when she broke records selling Mary Kay in the old days. We?

"I have fresh bagels in da car." This was so that we wouldn't be tempted to tear off an arm in hunger on the five-minute drive back to Auntie Eva's.

Kit grabbed my gear. Madison grabbed my arm. "See

you next practice," said Sarah as we made for the dressing
room.

"Tenk you, darrrlings! You are all so much to help, I tell
you true, tenk you!" Mama started backing up, waving and
blowing kisses at the same time. I don't know why I still get
surprised. But there she was blowing kisses like she was about
to disembark from the *Queen Mary,* and there's the rest of my
team blowing kisses right back.

Even the new assistant coach.

Like I said, she was *that* good.

In the end, there was a notice and a photograph in every single one of the papers. Only politicians and movie stars have their photos above their obituary. But there Luigi was in *The Globe and Mail,* the *Sun,* and the *Star*. Me and the Blondes worked out the wording and called it in that day we bolted from practice:

> *Prominent local businessman Luigi Pescatore died suddenly....*

Getting the relevant details from Auntie Eva was next to impossible as she swanned from room to room wailing and tearing at her clothes. I followed her around with pen in hand. He died the night before at her place but that was all I knew. "Uh, sorry, Auntie Eva, we, the papers, need to know what he, um, how he, uh, passed on?"

This unleashed a fresh torrent of piercing sobs. I honestly didn't know she liked him that much. In fact, I was pretty sure she didn't. Auntie Radmila grabbed my arm. "He died vit a smile on his face."

"Oh," I said, "uh, I don't think that we can put that in the paper."

"You tell zem," Auntie Luba said in between puffs of one of the three cigarettes she had going. "You tell zem it vas an attack in za heart!" She nodded, pleased with herself.

Prominent local businessman Luigi Pescatore died suddenly, but happily, of a heart attack....

"I don't know," I said. "I'm not sure that sounds ..."

"Iz perfect!" Auntie Eva wailed and then continued pacing.

"How about relatives?" asked Madison, scanning through the newspapers we had on hand. "These all say stuff like 'survived by' you know?"

"Pffftt." Auntie Eva waved her hand. "Zey vas so many times removed, zey disappeared. I vas his everyting." More wailing. Mama popped up to console her.

"It is not important," Mama whispered. "Da important ting is da picture." She glanced at her watch. "Papa vill be here soon. Ve sent him to buy da grieving food."

"That sounds great!" chirped Sarah.

Grieving food?

Prominent local business tycoon Luigi Pescatore died suddenly, but happily, on Thursday, September 9, 1976.

*Mr. Pescatore is survived by the love of his life, his
one and only, his most cherished and adored fiancée,
Miss ...*

Yes, Miss who? This prompted a rather intense debate.
Which of Auntie Eva's five possible last names were we going
to go with? Auntie Eva used her surnames like accessories.
She insisted between sobs that she liked the *sound* of her
second husband's name the most lately. So, even though Luigi
knew her best as *Eva Horvath, Kovach* it was. She sensibly
pointed out that it wasn't like Luigi was going to care.

*... Miss Eva Kovach. Service to be held at Our Lady of
Perpetual Sorrow, Saturday, September 11, at 10 A.M.*

The Aunties pronounced that version perfect. "Call it in,"
I said to Kit, who had taken the initiative to hunt down the
numbers for the obit/advertising sections of each newspaper.
Papa would drop off the accompanying photos as soon as he
got back with the food.

"So, back to the removed cousins," said Madison.

"Yoy, yoy!" Auntie Eva patted her chest and made for her
bedroom, with Mama hot on her heels.

"Sorry." Madison winced. Auntie Radmila and Auntie
Luba shrugged. "But maybe we have to try to find them for the
funeral at least and for, well, the will, and so on, you know?"

Mama came back while I was pouring coffee, and she
threw her arms around me. "Dey vas very, very, distantly
distant cousins."

"Mama, I'm pouring here."

"How do you know they were so distant, Mrs. Kandinsky?" asked Madison.

"Da lawyer," said Mama.

"Pa da," agreed Auntie Radmila, "za lawyer."

I put the carafe down. "What lawyer?"

"Za von vit za vill," said Auntie Luba sweetly.

"Well, that must have broken some land speed record." Kit shook her head.

"Formidable," agreed Madison, whose entire family, up and down both sides, were lawyers, law professors, judges, or all three.

"And …" I urged.

"He vas very fat," said Auntie Luba.

"Da!" nodded Auntie Radmila. "His feet vas very fat, he—"

"Guys!" I interrupted. "The will. Do we know what's going to happen?"

"Pa sure," shrugged Mama.

"Amazing," said Madison. "Grandfather will be stunned to hear how fast this went through."

"Ya, stunned! I don't know how za voman does it." Auntie Radmila went for the brandy bottle. "Luigi arranged for everyting. If za untinkable vas to be tinkable, he vanted his little jevel to be protected." The sobbing in the bedroom ratcheted up a notch at "little jevel."

"Wow," said Kit and Sarah at the same time. "So what did she get?"

No one was startled or offended. It was a perfectly decent question at least in this company.

"So, he left his little house in Little Italy to za removable cousins, Maria and Mario." Auntie Radmila downed her brandy in one go. "Zen, za business, Pescatore's White Night Limos vit za tree black cars and za super stretchy vite von, all his investments, his cash monies … all goes to Eva!" She poured another shot. "It's crazy! Za voman is already a multi-millionaire from za ozer dead and divorced husbands. She didn't even have to marry zis von!"

"I'm hearing zat, Radmila!" came a warning shot from the bedroom.

At least she'd stopped crying.

"I'm telling you true!" countered Auntie Radmila. "My tongue should fall out and I should step on it if I lie!"

Sarah flinched at the image.

"But … she doesn't even drive," I said. "How can she run a limo company?"

Mama shrugged. "Vat can I say? Da voman has a gift."

Auntie Eva emerged from the bedroom fairly dry, but her beehive was askew.

Papa blew in just then. I flashed him a massive smile. A big part of that smile was a coded but compelling message reminding him to come home soon. We've been talking about subliminal messages in English this term and I've been practising the smile ever since. It's a damn good smile. Frankly, I don't understand why he hasn't moved back yet, especially since I noticed that Mama was offering up the same smile. Mama didn't need a class on subliminal anything.

Mama helped Papa unload two shopping bags brimming with kielbasas, salamis, smoked meats, olives, pickles, rye and corn breads, and a half a dozen cheeses. They looked so right unpacking together. It was brilliant to see, even though they didn't talk much. They probably didn't have to. Long-standing deep love is like that. Someone on the CBC said so just last week. Papa waved at the Blondes, kissed me, grabbed the photos for the papers, righted Auntie Eva's beehive, and was off.

"Who was that masked man?" I asked.

"Zat vas your Papa, you funny-pants girl," smiled Auntie Luba. "He is very too busy. He must to go to za florist, za church, za funeral home, za newspapers, et cetera, et cetera, et cetera."

"Uh, how is he doing all of this?" I asked. The Blondes were already in the kitchen looking for platters to present the food.

"Vit von of za black limousines," shrugged Auntie Eva. "He has a list."

Kit came in with the cheeses, Sarah had two plates full of the pickles and breads, and Madison held the biggest platter heaping with smoked meats.

"Good girls." Mama patted Sarah's cheek. "You learn vell."

Wait a second. "But, guys ... unless he got it while he was in prison, Papa does not have a driver's licence!" Why was I the only one who ever thought of these things?

Madison's eyes widened. Even Kit looked impressed as she gnawed on a slice of salami.

"Pshhhaw," said Auntie Radmila as she went for the cheese plate. "Your Papa vas a very good driver in Poland, in Yugoslavia, in Hungary, in every place."

"Ya," snorted Auntie Eva, "especially ven he vas sober."

"Okay, and while that's good, the thing is, see, he still doesn't have his—"

"Let it go." Madison patted my hand. Kit nodded.

Jesus God, I was getting Auntie advice from the Blondes. It was like being dropped headfirst into an alternative universe.

We spent the next hour sorting out the details of the funeral. I kept taking notes. I should have felt worse than I did, really. Worse for Auntie Eva and definitely worse for poor old Luigi. But then again, I hardly knew him. Still, a good, religious-type person would have felt worse. Instead, I'm ashamed to say, I felt kind of important. We decided that there were going to be no viewings. Auntie Eva said she'd had enough of viewing dead husbands and lovers. The church, however, had to be covered in white gardenias and white roses.

"Wow, that's so sweet," said Sarah. "His favourite flowers?"

"No darling," she tweaked Sarah's cheek, "mine. He liked carnations like our Sophie. Carnations!" She shuddered. "I ask you?" Sympathetic shuddering from the Aunties and Madison.

It was going to be a full Catholic mass. "Sophie, you vas baptized Catolic," Auntie Eva announced. "And you vent to za Catolic schools two times. You must talk to za priest, okay?"

"Me? But I don't actually have any Catholic training, remember? We lied to them about that part to get me into those schools!"

Silence.

"No first communion, no confirmation …" I really don't know why I bothered.

More silence.

"I don't even remember how to fake being Catholic!"

No one said anything at all for a very long time. Many silent seconds ticked by.

"Fine, I'll go talk to the priest."

Auntie Eva snatched me into a massive smother hug.

More God stuff.

"And say zat you are Luigi's niece," said Auntie Eva.

"You want me to lie? Outright? To a priest?"

"Pa da," said Auntie Radmila.

"But it's the Catholic church!"

"Exactly," sniffed Auntie Eva. "You know how zey are, unless you are a good Catolic, zey vill never cooperate. Ve are not related vit poor Luigi, and he vas such a big Catolic." She paused here for a moment while we watched her eyes well up again. "You vant ve should bury him in a ditch?"

"Well no, geez," I moaned. "Of course not. I guess." Unbelievable, I was right back to lying my face off to Catholic clergy. "When?"

"Oooh!" Auntie Eva glanced at her watch and hustled over with my jacket. "You must go right avay fast to talk to za priest. Fazer Gregory in za church around za block is expecting you zis minute. Our Lady of Perpetual Sobbing."

"Sorrow!" I said, even though she was grieving and everything.

"Zat is vat I said!" She blew her nose. "Mainly. Ven your

head is full of sobbing your heart is full of sorrow, and za Catolics know zis."

We all nodded like that was a comprehensible sentence and everything.

I was hustled out of Auntie Eva's and found myself in the vestibule of Our Lady of Perpetual Sorrow before I really knew what had happened. The church was empty, just me and all those statues and stained glass. It felt good. Lazy afternoon sunrays snuck through the clear bits in the windows, warming the carved oak and playing with decades of dust. Without thinking, I dipped my fingers into the font of holy water. I was eleven again. I made the sign of the cross, walked toward the altar, genuflected in front of the tabernacle, and slid into the first pew like I had just done it last Sunday. It was scary how it all came back. My breathing slowed. I remembered this part; it always made me feel pure and righteous. Maybe I could be a Catholic after all. I knew a fair bit from faking it all those years. I heard footsteps. A priest approached me from one of the confessional boxes.

"My child." He smiled. "I am Father Gregory."

"Hi Father, I believe you were expecting me. I'm Sophie Pescatore." I snuck a peek back at the confessional box, remembering the clean feeling I'd get after confession. The nuns all assumed I'd had my first communion and I never corrected them. I loved confession and confessing. I was a first-class confessor. And, apparently, I was still a first-class liar, except now, I felt bad about it. Father Gregory held out his hand.

"Yeah, so, uh, I'm Luigi's niece, here to discuss my dearly, uh, departed and beloved uncle's funeral service."

Maybe there was some other looser, more Sophie-suitable type of religion that understood about the necessity of fabrications and falsehoods. I decided to wait for a sign from God on that one.

"So, Father, thing is, my uncle loved white roses and gardenias ..."

5

"Oh, Lord," I said to no one in particular as I clambered into the far end of the limo. "You've got to admit that this is weird, even for us." We were off to Luigi's funeral mass. I knocked on the window separating the driver from the passengers. It slid open. "Papa, do you even know how to drive this thing?"

"It's a car." He shrugged.

Mama, Auntie Eva, and Auntie Luba were in pride of place in the back seat, with Auntie Radmila and Uncle Dragan opposite them. The man hadn't said a word in years, but he exuded an air of contentment that wafted off him in visible waves. Every time I saw him, I was reminded that there must be more to Auntie Radmila than meets the eye. Mike, and I could not bring myself to call him "uncle" since he was still my employer at the restaurant, Mike sat shotgun with Papa to keep him company and help him guess at what all the buttons were for. The dashboard looked like Command and Control for North American Air Defense.

I tucked myself in beside Auntie Radmila so I could keep tabs on the driver. Uncle Dragan tapped a button on the black console and, presto, produced a stash of brandy stored in a beautiful cut-glass decanter. He also whipped out six gorgeous little crystal glasses and started pouring. Everybody but Papa had a glass. Even Mama.

"Živili!" Mike lifted his glass, which was barely visible in his big meaty paw.

"To life!" I agreed and immediately wondered whether that was entirely appropriate given the circumstances.

We clinked glasses and downed our brandy in one gulp. The brandy went straight to my head, and I made a conscious decision to regard our outrageous little procession with a mellower eye. It didn't help.

All of us wore black from head to toe. We were black on black and still we were too colourful. How was that even possible? I turned back to the driver. "Could we at least do something about the lights?" Somehow, either Papa or Mike had hit a bad button, so now, not only were we going to a funeral in a white super stretch with twinkle lights, but the stupid twinkle lights were flashing non-stop. I'd never been to a funeral mass before, but I just knew twinkling twinkle lights couldn't be right. It didn't seem to bother anyone else.

"I just don't know what we did there, Princess." Papa squinted at the dashboard. "It's okay though. I think Luigi would be pleased."

Jesus God, after six months of living in her basement apartment, Papa was thinking like Auntie Eva, a textbook case of Stockholm syndrome.

"Absolutely, Slavko darling!" Auntie Eva held up her glass for a refill.

Slavko *darling*?

Everyone had a refill. Including Mama and including—when Mama was busy comforting Auntie Eva—me. I inhaled that shot too. At this rate, we were going to pour ourselves half-loaded out of the car like a group of kids on their way to prom. In my defence, I argued for decorum every step of the way. It was me who said we should use two of Luigi's lovely black limos. That was hotly voted down by Mama and Auntie Eva, who felt that we should all be together during this searingly tragic moment. Besides, they felt that the white limo with the twinkle lights was more festive.

You'd think I'd recognize defeat when it landed in my lap, but I pressed on to my next agenda item. "Papa?"

"Yes, Princess?"

"I know I've said it before, but shouldn't you wait to drive this thing until you maybe got your licence or something?"

Everybody, including Papa, turned to me and smiled.

"What?"

"You say, Eva."

"No, Slavko." Auntie Eva smiled sweetly. "You go ahead."

It was official. Their cold war had melted over Luigi's dead body. They had hated each other for my entire life. Papa felt that Auntie Eva was a lying, scheming, manipulative busybody. Auntie Eva, on the other hand, kept playing the prison/drunk card on Papa. And now here they were ready to go on tour together.

"What?" I repeated.

"Well, kid." Mike cleared his throat. "I pulled a few strings …"

Mike's strings were legendary. They went from behind his restaurant counter all the way to the premier's office and got tied into knots throughout the city. It never ceased to shock me. The guy was like a combination short-order cook and Balkan warlord. Square-chested gentlemen, who rumbled when they talked, often turned up near the end of my shift on Saturdays and sat on the very last stool on the counter. They always wore suits, always ordered coffee, and always over-tipped. I loved them.

"And …" Mike turned around to make sure everyone was paying attention. "And your pops should have his licence by the end of next week."

"And?" Auntie Eva patted my knee, beaming.

Mike lit a cigarette and offered them around. It took a few minutes for the cigarettes to be lit and then, of course, the glasses had to be refilled.

"And …" I said.

"And as soon as he's got that under his belt and the lawyers have worked it out all legal like." He paused to blow a few smoke rings. "Then your Papa will be the new president and chief executive officer of Pescatore's White Night Limousine Service!"

The back of the limo erupted into squealing, clapping, and hollering. "Wait, but what about Auntie Eva?"

"Eva is the chairman, of course," said Papa.

Of course.

We resumed squealing.

"Eva." Mama's eyes welled up. "Eva, how can I …" She put a hand to her throat. "I, how …"

"Phooey!" Auntie Eva downed her brandy. "I need somevone I could trust. Tycoons need peoples. Besides, it vould make Luigi happy."

I hoped Luigi knew how happy he was.

"May God have a rest on his soul." Auntie Luba made the sign of the cross. They all made the sign of the cross. For people who hadn't set foot in a church since my baptism, they sure were getting their Catholic on. I couldn't blame them; it was all enough to make you believe in God whether you wanted to or not. Papa had more or less been out of work since he got out of prison last year. He'd gone from jobless to president in a week *and* he was sober! At this rate he'd be back home by the weekend.

We all filed into the church, trying to look sombre. Auntie Eva got into the moment as soon as she saw the coffin, laden with gardenias and a few stray white carnations. She turned around and whispered, "Ver did za carnations come from? I said roses and gardenias!" Then she promptly threw herself on said carnations and gardenias. "*Yoy!* Luigi, my love, my everyting!" She pounded on the apparently suitable cherry veneer coffin. "How could you leave your little dumpling?" Sob, sob. "Lord, take me instead!" Auntie Luba waited for a beat then took the prostrate Auntie Eva to the front pew, where she draped herself onto me, inconsolable.

Nobody orchestrates like the Aunties; it's a DNA thing. Everyone, friend, foe, or family, must know that Luigi would be missed, Luigi would be mourned.

I looked around as soon as my head was free.

"How many?" she whispered.

"More than thirty, less than fifty."

"Not bad. I asked za ladies from za Hungarian Hall to come and cry."

"I see them in the middle of the church, on our side."

"Vat are zey doing?"

"Crying."

"You call zat crying? Zat is not crying! Zat is sniffling! I asked for crying!"

The Blondes were there, in the third row, along with Madison's grandfather, the Judge. He probably drove them over. Madison got a brand-new car for her sixteenth birthday, but she had just flunked her driver's licence test for the third time last week. She may have to get fixed up by Mike, too. There were various odds and sods of people and then a man and a woman who looked eerily alike in the "family" pew opposite us.

I nudged Auntie Radmila in the ribs and mouthed, "Who are they?"

"Za removable cousins," Auntie Radmila whispered so loud that the entire church turned to look at the distantly removed cousins. Mario and Maria sat all by themselves, swallowed up by the dark oak pew. The Aunties had much remarked upon the singularity of Luigi's Italian ancestry. Neither he nor Mario nor Maria had ever been married or had children.

"It's not natural for an Italian," Auntie Luba complained.

People kept coming. A very old couple were followed by a few people who may have been Luigi's regular clients, who were followed by, Jesus God, Mr. Wymeran, five girls from our second string, and … David! I whipped around and stared at the coffin. Luckily, the funeral procession started and Auntie Eva had sprung for a soloist, so I got distracted. Still, *he* was back there. What was he doing here? *Concentrate.* I was up soon with the First Reading. I settled into the comforting ritual of it all. I'd forgotten how much I had enjoyed Catholic ceremonies, the hymns, the incense, the readings … it was just like an AA meeting, except that it was me going up to the podium and all eyes would be on me. I liked that too. The reading was from Corinthians 13:1–13, the bit about love. It might make Luigi happy.

"If I speak in the tongues of mortals and angels …"

It was a nice turnout after all. I looked out at everyone. Auntie Eva needn't have fretted so much. I felt David's eyes on me. Why was he here? I looked back at my text.

"Love is always patient and kind; love is never jealous …"

As I read, the hairs on the front of my arms burned and bristled.

"Love never ends …" I went through the rest of that beautiful reading and finally looked up and all the way to the back of the church. A solitary figure stood in silhouette at the entrance. My heart lurched. I glanced back at the fourth row. No. David was still sitting there.

Luke.

I swear it was Luke. How did he know? Why was he here?

I stepped down and turned to go into the aisle and then looked back again. Gone. But it *was* him. It was! The air had been charged with electricity and now it wasn't. It was always like that with Luke. I turned back one more time. No. Second Reading, Gospel Acclamation, Gospel Reading, Homily, Hymns, Communion and, through it all, I could feel that Luke *was* there and now he wasn't. His absence was a physical thing.

It was a beautiful sermon, someone snuck carnations onto the coffin, *and* Luke Pearson had come! Luke in a church! Talk about your sign from God!

6

About four pews' worth of mourners exited the church and regrouped at the Mount Pleasant Cemetery with decorum and dignity. We weren't one of them.

Mike and Uncle Dragan were weaving by the time we got out of the limo again, and Papa looked like he needed a drink. Auntie Eva artfully kept up the waterworks throughout the interment and the prayers, joined for brief sobbing serenades by Aunties Luba and Radmila and even Mama. I was sure Auntie Eva was going to pitch herself on top of the coffin when we got to the "ashes to ashes" part.

I nudged Auntie Luba. "Is she okay? Maybe we should—"

"Shhht." Auntie Luba put a finger to her mouth. "Za more she cries, za less she is going to have to pee."

"Uh … pardon?"

"Ya," she snorted. "She's got on a girdle zat takes two peoples to get her into. Let her cry."

Mama leaned over. "She's right. Eva looks fantastik, but it's very impossible to get zat girdle off."

"It's too tight," sniffed Auntie Radmila. "Zat's vhy she is crying so much."

I'm ashamed to say I hardly thought about poor old Luigi. Yet another tick in the "why I'm not nice" column, especially when I so wanted to be "nice." It's like a long-standing goal and everything. I *wanted* to feel awful about him dying, but I didn't. Even worse, they'd just been together for a few months, so I had a limited bank of "treasured" memories to call up to make me feel teary when everyone was looking. I mean, I knew he adored Auntie Eva, but there was a shockingly long lineup of men who did, including all her ex-husbands. To complicate matters further, Luigi's dying gave Papa his first real job in decades. It all got kind of sticky if I thought about it too much.

So I stopped thinking about it.

Therefore, when I wasn't interrupted by Auntie Eva's gut-cleansing sobs, my thoughts were free to go straight to Luke. I thought intelligent, deep thoughts like: Was that really Luke? Maybe it wasn't. But then again, I had that whole electric thing. It sure looked like Luke. But then again, it was just his silhouette. It probably wasn't him. But then again, I bet it was. I was making myself carsick.

Then we went back to the car.

The mourners all came to Auntie Eva's too. Father Gregory made it sound like it was pretty well mandatory. Auntie Eva stopped sobbing the moment she got into the limo and did not cry again. In fact, most of the trip home was devoted to makeup repair. Mike had taken care of the catering, but not from his restaurant, mind you. We all agreed that burgers and fries didn't hit the right note. He arranged for lasagne and veal Parmesan, Luigi's favourite meal, because, of course, it would make Luigi happy.

To make the rest of us happy, Mike got his two studly nephews, whom we'd met at his wedding, to help serve, get drinks, and flirt with my friends. "Oooo," said Sarah as soon as she spotted Mike Jr. and George in their waiter outfits.

"Down, girl." Kit yanked her back. "Let's remember those boys are in their twenties and you took an abstinence pledge, right?" Sarah groaned by way of an answer. Mike Jr. was stationed at Auntie Eva's dining room table handing out plates and urging people to load up, while George cajoled people into ordering drinks. Or maybe it was the other way around. I could never remember which one was which.

Papa was in the kitchen whipping up his new favourite thing in the world, milkshakes. What Papa gave up in alcohol, he replaced by mainlining chocolate malteds. Mama kept giving him her best subliminal smile, but it didn't look like they were getting much of a chance to talk and catch up.

Auntie Eva made her way straight to the big red-velvet wing chair in the living room. This is where she would *receive*. "Buboola," she said, her arm outstretched to me, "come." It was a little awkward. Auntie Eva sat in the chair, of course, but she also insisted that I sit. So, I perched precariously on the arm of the chair, trying to look graceful, secure, and suitably stricken as people made their way over, one by one.

"Straighten up," she whispered. "Nobody can see your breasts ven you are hunching over like zat."

I straightened up.

Mario and Maria made their way over with drinks in hand. They expressed their deep Italian gratitude that Auntie Eva had organized such a lovely send-off for their cousin.

"Pshaw." Auntie Eva waved her hanky at them. "Vat are you talking. I ashamed of zis poultry effort!"

They looked alarmed.

"Paltry," I whispered.

"Zat is vat I said," she said without breaking eye contact with them. This is where the cousins were supposed to insist that they had never seen a finer or more impressive funeral in their lives. Instead they shook her hand and drifted to the food table.

"Peasants," muttered Auntie Eva before she was assaulted by the Blondes. Kit, Sarah, and Madison all threw themselves at her. "It was brilliant!" said Sarah.

"*You* look brilliant!" said Kit.

"It's all too tragic for words," sighed Madison.

"Absolutely!" they all said. "You poor, poor thing." More hugging. Hankies were prominently waved about. Then they hugged her again.

You can't teach this stuff. You either pick it up or you don't. I had never been prouder of them.

"He's right behind us," Madison whispered, while giving me a condolence hug.

"Huh? Who?" I said.

"Just look sexy!"

"Breasts, breasts!" hissed Auntie Eva.

I inhaled, thrust out my chest, and tried to cross my legs artfully like they show you in *Cosmopolitan* magazine. Right over left, but high so your flabby fat thigh isn't pressed against anything and your legs are super e-l-o-n-g-a-t-e-d. It was not a move designed for the sculpted arm of a velvet wing chair. My butt rolled right off the edge. Just before I hit the floor, I was scooped up by one arm. Wow. I looked up.

Damn.

Double damn.

It was David.

"My goodness pieces!" Auntie Eva fanned herself with her hanky. "So strong vit za muscles and so very beautiful too. Sophie, my little carnation, who loves carnations ve don't know vhy, my Sophie tenks you very much for saving her from za floor." She elbowed me.

I elbowed her back. Actually, I wanted to kill her, but I settled for duelling elbows. "Uh, yeah." Okay, this was awkward. I could tell she'd decided to love David unconditionally. I knew all the signs. "Auntie Eva, you remember David Walter?" I psychically drilled into her brain that he hated my guts for some unjustifiable reason and therefore she must give him the coldest of cold shoulders, freeze him out, and cut him down.

"Velcome, velcome! Za boy vit za two first names!" She took his hand and put hers on top of his. "I remember you, of course, except you are even more fantastik zan my remembering! A movie star, eh, Sophie?"

"Yeah, movie star."

Two bright red patches splashed David's cheeks. The unflappable David Walter looked flapped. What the hell was he doing here anyway? Did he come on a bet? Guys do stuff like that.

"I was at the practice when …"

"Oh you are za coach! *Da,* Magda told it to me. How fantastik for Sophie and your team too, of course. Ve are all vaiting vit bated breasts."

Dear Lord. My face felt like I was standing in front of a furnace. Move over, Luigi. I'll be there in a minute.

David, thank God, looked lost. And because I simply could not stop myself, I said, "Bated *breath*."

She patted his hand and through a clenched smile said, "Zat is vat I said."

"Well, I'm very sorry for your loss, ma'am." He turned to me. All six-foot-four inches of him looked seismically uncomfortable. "And for you, Sophie, for the loss of your, uh, um, well … uncle?"

"Uncle will do," I said to put him out of his misery, which I thought was very *nice* of me.

"Okay, well, my condolences to you both then." He backed away like his butt was on fire. Seriously, *what* did I ever do to him?

"Za boy is completely koo-koo for you!" said Auntie Eva before she was smothered by a Hungarian couple.

"Yeah," I said, "that's pretty obvious."

Auntie Eva greeted every guest like they had scaled Mount Everest to reach her with their condolences. The food kept coming and the drinks didn't stop flowing. The Blondes were singing and swaying to Auntie Eva's collection of Dean Martin records because it *would've made Luigi happy.* Papa was on his fourth milkshake and even convinced the Judge, Madison's grandfather, to have one before he left. Although the Judge was responsible for getting Papa exonerated and freed from prison, he also had a bit of a crush on Mama stemming back from the days when he thought she was a widow. But there they were, in the Auntie universe, side by each, sipping their chocolate malteds.

I eventually left with Madison and her grandfather. Sarah and Kit stayed behind. Sarah to keep flirting with George and Kit to keep an eye on Sarah's flirting.

"Your mother looked lovely, as always," the Judge said as we got into his Mercedes.

Eeew … what are you supposed to say to that? Adults are so weird. I wanted to say, "Back off, mister. They're separated, *not* divorced. My mother is still in love with the guy you were sipping shakes with!"

Instead, I said, "Yes, sir."

Madison, who was in the back with me, squeezed my hand. "Do you want me to come up with you?" she whispered. "I don't think you should be alone."

What the hell? "No, I'm cool, thanks though." Madison knew I wasn't all torn up about poor Luigi. "I'm going to do the laundry, to tell you the truth. With all of this drama, I won't have anything to wear to school next week unless I start now."

She leaned in close. "I saw him too."

We didn't say anything from Davenport Road to Mount Pleasant Road. We'd been through too much together. I didn't insult her by asking who. Papa always said to never kid a kidder, and Madison was among the best. "It's okay." I kept her gaze. "I'll be okay."

She nodded reluctantly, not quite believing. That's the other thing about us, all of us: although we trust each other, we don't always *believe* each other.

"I really do have a big pile and I like being in the laundry room by myself with the chugging of the machines. It helps me think, calms me down, you know?"

Madison had no idea what a washing machine looked like, let alone sounded like, but she nodded again anyway. "Okay, but call me if you need me, if you want to talk."

As soon as I got in I threw all my clothes into the laundry hamper, and, in an act of unspeakable generosity, I threw in Mama's too.

The laundry room was relentlessly cheerful, covered in blindingly white subway tiles and decorated with five massive white washing machines and five equally massive and gleaming white dryers. The magic chugging of the machines wasn't working though. Not this time. I still felt agitated and antsy.

David turning up was bad enough, but Luke? I was blind-sided by Luke. Why did Luke come to the church? I paced a zigzag route in between the washers and dryers. That didn't do it either. We were all by ourselves, the machines and me. "I need some answers here. Help!" I begged the laundry room.

And the laundry room answered.

After throwing the first load into the dryer, I wandered over to the laundry room's famous collection of used books and magazines. It was a stellar, if wonky, stash. My hand went straight to the biggest book, the one with the shiny black cover under the *True Confessions* and dated *Cosmopolitan*s.

Chugga shoosh, chugga shoosh, chugga—

Oh my God! I clutched the book to my chest. In a day bursting with signs, here was another one, straight from God to me. How could it not be? I was holding something called *The Concise Encyclopaedia of Living Faiths*! Here was my *something,* somewhere in this book of religions. Last year when I was walking into walls all confused about sex and how to be a *woman,* I got all my questions answered in a book Auntie Eva brought over called *Sweet Savage Love* by Rosemary Rogers. It was my bible on love. Now, I needed a new bible, maybe a Bible bible to get me through the bad bits. Clearly, God needed me to choose a religion and then He would make everything better. My life would be a daily dose of miracles. All I had to do was pick one! How clear was that? How brilliant was that? Hell, I bet they make a movie about this moment one day.

I was busy arranging my freshly laundered clothes on the floor of my room when Kit buzzed in. I glanced at the clock: 8:38 P.M. It already felt like the world's longest day and the funeral party could go on for still hours more.

"Hey, how's it going?" she asked, breezing into the condo.

"Okay." I was holding a neon green and orange T-shirt when I let her in. "What's up? Kit, you didn't leave Sarah alone with Mike Jr. and George, did you?"

"Oh ye of little faith," she snorted. "Don't you trust in our Sarah's pledge of celibacy, the one that she swore will restore and then retain her virginity until she's safely wed?"

I examined the T-shirt, ashamed of my suspicious self.

"Yeah, me neither." She slapped my back. "I just came from dropping her off. So what's up?"

"Uh, I'm just folding. It's a big deal with me." She looked confused. "You know, because I don't have a dresser or

58

anything. I have to fold and arrange my clothes just so on the floor."

She still looked blank so she headed off to my room. I followed her. What was up? "Wow, clothing as art," she said, admiring my convoluted little piles. "I keep forgetting you don't have any furniture." She shook her head. "You guys still saving or what?"

"No, it's me," I admitted. "I just can't get it together to fix it."

"Well hop to it, buttercup. You'll be off to university before you know it."

"Kit, I know you didn't come over to razz me about my room."

She threw herself onto my bed. "No." She waved at the laundry. "Pray continue, fair maiden."

I picked up where I left off with the T-shirt. The creases had to be just so. That way, when I put the other clothes on top, I never had to iron anything.

"You okay?" she asked.

"Me?"

"Yeah, you."

"Yeah, why? Are *you* okay?"

"You first."

So something *was* up. I watched Kit roll onto her back and investigate my beige ceiling.

"I'm cool, nothing special …"

"Yeah, yeah, yeah." She rolled back onto her stomach and looked at me. "I know the signs, remember? You're holding something, Soph. Tell me and I'll tell you."

She had me. I was officially worried. Kit was twisty. I mean more than usual. She knew I'd start freaking about whether she'd slipped back into her habit of puking on demand, so I coughed up. "Luke was at the church."

"Today? No guff." She bolted up and frowned. "I didn't see him."

"He was at the very back and he left early. Madison saw him too."

She grabbed a pair of jeans and started folding. "What the hell was he, is he, how dare he!" Then she seemed to remember I was there. "And?"

"And I'm good. I guess. A bit more stunned than usual, but that's just my life lately, you know?" Kit nodded and frowned at the same time. Was she worried about *me*? "But it's cool, you know why? I've decided to get some help from the big guy." I walked over to my mirror. "I'm going to get myself some religion." I liked how I looked when I said that.

"Religion?" I could see her in the mirror. She looked angry. "Religion, what the hell for?"

"I don't know." I shrugged, still tracking us in the mirror. "I just want more backup, you know?" I turned around. "I've been thinking about it ever since Mama, me, and the Aunties snuck into that AA meeting last month. The drunks might be on to something. You should've seen them, Kit." She was folding and refolding the same pair of jeans. Her attention to my creases was alarming. "Kit?"

"Religion will give you a rash," she said through gritted teeth. "It's for chumps. A waste of time. The only thing the Commies got right is that saying about how it's the 'opiate of the masses.'"

Whoa! "Okay, first of all. I don't like creases in my jeans."
She refolded them flat front without skipping a beat. "Second,
I don't mean religion with a capital R. Not Anglican like you
guys, or even Catholic like my old schools." The memory of
lying to Father Gregory pricked me. "Definitely not Catholic.
Just some nice, cool, laid-back religion that I can pull out of
my pocket when I need it, you know?"

"There's no such thing, Soph!" Why was she so cranked
up? "Religions are anti-everything, anti-life. It's just rules. If
you want to feel like a sinner, if you want to feel like a freak,
by all means, get yourself a religion. Even my shrink says—"

"No, Kit. I said I'm not going to pick one of those!" I
snatched my jeans back. "I'm going to get a mellow one, like
the Beatles and yoga."

"Okay, that's an exercise not a religion."

"You know what I mean—that Indian stuff, with the sitars.
Maybe I'll even pick a couple and blend them. It's all in my
book here." I tossed her the encyclopedia. "I started reading
it in the laundry room. I mean if a bunch of stoners like the
Beatles found a religion to like …"

Kit didn't even glance at the cover before dropping it back
into the laundry basket. "Well, so long as you're okay." She
looked at her watch. "Damn, I've got to go. Dad needs the car
back like half an hour ago." She bolted through the living room
and was almost to the door before I realized she was going.

"Wait, Kit!" I was still holding the stupid jeans. "I told.
You said that you would tell. Something's up. What's up?"

Her back was to me, but I could still see her tense up.
"Later."

The door swung open. "Hello, Princess!" Papa beamed at me. "And my Princess's beautiful left guard!"

"Aw, you always know what to say to a girl, Mr. Kandinsky." She grabbed the door from him. "Catch you guys later."

As Papa headed for the kitchen and the Turkish coffee utensils, I trotted out to the elevators after Kit. She had just stepped in and hit G. "Relax, sweetcheeks, I'm not puking." She put her hand on her heart just as the doors were closing. "I swear."

Okay. What then?

"Did I chase her away?" called Papa from the kitchen.

"No, Papa, she had to get the car back." He came over and kissed my forehead.

"How's Auntie Eva and everyone back at the party?" I asked.

"It's just the hard core and, oh, Mario and Maria are still there too. They were singing Luigi's favourite soccer songs as I was leaving."

"Even Mama?"

"Even your Mama." He smiled and kissed me again. "Eva is putting on the show of her life for those two cousins." He poured himself a shot of the dark black liquid and held up the carafe to me. I snuggled into the image of having him back in the kitchen, back at home where he belonged. But *why* was he at home where he belonged?

"No thanks, Papa, I'm all coffeed out. So …?"

I watched him squint at the laundry basket. "I could not do one more milkshake. I just needed a minute away from all that, well …"

"Brandy?"

"Yes, I needed a breather from all that brandy." He smiled like he was sharing a joke with himself. And I just wanted to see you, too, without drama. He picked up my book. *"The Concise Encyclopaedia of Living Faiths?"*

"Yeah, cool, isn't it? I found it in the laundry room, I've been thinking of dabbling in a bit of religion and then, presto, God leaves me his holy encyclopedia in the laundry room! Talk about a miracle, eh?"

Unlike Kit, Papa didn't look so much alarmed as amused. "Well, Princess, last year it was all that purple prose and romance, so why not a spiritual quest this year?"

Papa got it. Papa always got it, got me. I felt the punch of missing him all over again, even though he was sitting right there.

He ran his finger down the index page.

"It's probably a phase, typical teenage individuation," I said.

He raised an eyebrow.

"It means separating from your parental units. We learned about it in guidance. Or it could just be plain old rebellion, given that you and Mama are such surefire atheists." I watched for his reaction given what I now knew about the Twelve Steps.

"Nothing is for sure." He grabbed my hand and squeezed it. "That's the only thing an alcoholic knows for sure."

I wanted to ask when does an alcoholic know for sure that he's no longer an alcoholic, and when does that alcoholic then come home for good and make everything normal again?

Instead I said, "I skimmed Zoroastrians on page 209, which sounds like a real blast."

"I agree," he said when he flipped to the page. "Very swashbuckling. It must be the Zoro part."

"Yeah, but difficult for Toronto. See, thing is, when you die, you need this special structure called the Tower of Silence. Look at page 215."

We examined the photo. Papa whistled. "That's fantastic!"

"Yeah, so when you die your body is put in there and then it's picked apart by vultures and the rest decomposes by using this special stuff and your ashes, or remains, or whatever, return to the earth all pure."

"Vultures!" He scanned the pages. "Definitely pick this one."

"Can't. I bet we don't have a single Tower of Silence in the whole city, and you can't just whip one up, you know?"

"I see your problem, especially since the Tower is probably the most compelling part for you, right?"

"Right!" I took the book back.

"I see your dilemma." He pulled me over and kissed my forehead again. "But, let's face it, you are at the very beginning of your search. I know of poets who search their entire lives for the meaning of God."

"Yeah, well, I'm giving myself a week," I said.

"Seems reasonable." He nodded absently. I'd lost him. "So ... how is she?"

"Who?" I asked.

"Your Mama." He poked me. "Who else?"

"Well, you see her ... you just saw her!"

"Sure, but I mean really, is she okay?"

I thought about all those weekends shut away. I closed my encyclopedia. "Papa, separating parents should not be putting their vulnerable offspring in the middle of these awkward situations with these awkward-type questions."

"Guidance again?"

I nodded. It was actually a whole session devoted to *divorcing* parents, but I wasn't about to plant that little seed.

"Sounds like a hell of a class!" He threw his arm around me. "Well, I better be getting back to my happily inebriated mourners and see who I should be driving home. Oh the irony, eh, Princess?" He winked.

I wanted to beg him to stay, plead with him to stop leaving, for God's sake. *I can keep you sober here! I'll do it this time. Promise.* Instead, I just got up. "I'll walk you to the elevator, Papa." We strolled elegantly, arm in arm, into the hallway, and I blew back kisses when he threw them to me from inside the elevator. There. See. That's better. How mature was that? I was sixteen now after all. I felt very composed, very controlled, and—as soon as the doors shut—very alone.

8

Kit smacked the back of my head as I slid into our booth at Mike's.

"Ow!"

"What the hell did you do to that boy?" she demanded. "And more importantly, can you stop doing it? I mean fourteen suicides, Sophie. Geez!"

"I know," I moaned. "I've been telling you guys for days, but you wouldn't believe me."

"Well, I believe you now." Madison winced as she pulled herself into the seat. "He hates you all right."

"Who hates my Sophie?" asked Mike as he came over with our standing order for post-practice coffee and fries. "I'll kill the bum."

"David Walter," Kit volunteered. "Our new assistant coach. He made us all do like ten extra suicides and blamed Sophie for every one. 'You are outta shape, Ms. Kandinsky, which means your team is outta shape. Assume the position!'"

We all winced. It was a good imitation.

"But he's just conflicted is all," insisted Sarah.

"He hates her all right," said Kit.

"Naw!" snorted Mike. "He don't hate Sophie. Nobody could hate Sophie." Mike wandered back to the grill to throw on some buttered Danish, which we used as a chips-and-gravy chaser.

"No offence, Soph." Madison leaned over. "But the Aunties have got to him. Mike used to be razor sharp in the character assessment department."

Kit nodded and called out to Mike. "David is a senior. He played some football, but his real thing is basketball and he was best friends with—"

"I know who the kid is." Mike flipped the Danish onto an already heaping plate and plopped it onto our table. "And he don't hate our Sophie."

I was too tired and sore to argue. As soon as he left I said, "I think Auntie Luba has messed with his mind."

"Stands to reason," nodded Madison. "You'd think Coach would—"

"Coach?" Kit reached for a Danish. "Coach is happier than a pig in poo. He never would have got us in such good shape. Speaking of which, anyone got a cigarette? I'm out." Madison and Kit whipped out their packs.

What had I ever done to him? I was playing my guts out at every practice and he barely looked at me.

"What is it, Soph? You're not here with us," Kit said, lighting up. Even Sarah lit up. I hadn't seen her smoke since she'd quit last year when she thought she was pregnant. I watched her inhale. For the millionth time, I thought about smoking. "No, I am, I am … it's just that I was thinking … maybe it has something to do with Luke, right? I mean, we were a big secret, except that a lot of people were in on it when you stop and think about it. There's you guys and your families, the Aunties, Mama and Papa, and Mike, and maybe Luke told him, so, well, maybe David knew and is blaming me for Luke, or he's pissed about Luke two-timing Alison, or ... I don't know."

The Blondes nodded as if I had just said something that other English speakers would recognize.

Luke again. What was he doing in that church? Why did he come? How did he know? Did David tell him? It was as bad as before. I couldn't stop thinking about him. Maybe he couldn't stop thinking of me. Maybe …

"… just lucky you're still captain," Madison was saying.

"That's just because he hasn't worked out how to annul the vote," offered Kit. "Figure him out, Soph, or you won't last the season."

Thankfully we moved on to the next order of business, which was whether Madison should continue seeing Billy Wainright or not. Billy was the captain of the Lawrence Heights football team. This was all well and good image-wise, but it was a logistical nightmare for Madison, and by extension, us. Since Billy was captain, Madison, as the official girlfriend, had to put in an appearance at least at Lawrence's home games, plus, because of our position in our school, we had to attend all our home games, plus there were all our practices and then, for a brief period, an overlap of our actual basketball games. As nuts as this was, apparently that wasn't the real problem.

"The real problem …" we all leaned in, "is the way he kisses." Madison made a very unbecoming gagging sound.

"What?" asked Kit. "A slobberer? Don't tell me he slobbers!"

"I hate slobberers!" commiserated Sarah.

I nodded with disgusted empathy, even though I didn't know what I was nodding about. I have only ever been kissed by Luke. The gruesome Ferguson Englehardt, who back in grade nine spent an entire party trying to part my teeth with his tongue, did not count. No, there was just Luke. Luke and me, outside on the fire escape at Auntie Luba's wedding … Jesus God, I still wore his kisses, still felt them. I could taste Lucas Pearson even now, sitting there with my coffee. I shivered but kept nodding.

"He doesn't slobber." Madison lowered her voice. "He sucks."

"Yeah," nodded Kit. "I figured, but why?"

"No, I mean literally, he sucks."

"Ohhh …" nodded Sarah while keeping an eye out for Mike. "He's a Hoover."

Madison nodded. Everyone else made a face.

I couldn't pretend a minute longer. "I don't get it," I said.

"I keep forgetting that your education was pathetically lacking in all things important before us." Kit rolled her eyes.

"A Hoover," explained Sarah, "is one of the worst."

"Yup." Madison made a face. "It's like he's vacuuming your mouth, trying to suck out all your spit and your tongue."

I felt my gorge rise and my gag reflex signal danger.

"But, then again," Sarah came in to review the damage, "Billy is such a hunk, rival team captain, and ..."

"Then, when he gets tired from all that Hoovering," Madison raised her trump card, "he sticks his tongue right in and then, *then* he just leaves it there for a little rest."

"Whoa, stop!" Kit glanced my way. "Sophie's going to puke."

Sarah passed me some water. "Oh well, dump him then," she sighed. "You can't rehabilitate a tired tongue. We'll dig up someone from our own senior team for you. We can't have you with a Hooverer and a tongue-rester for heaven's sake."

They nodded. I burped.

By the time we left, it was dark. I went home with Madison. She needed moral reinforcement because Edna was invited for dinner. Madison still wasn't handling the whole Edna being her *real* biological grandmother any better. In fact, she was getting worse. Last year, she actually introduced Edna to Kit as her former housekeeper, which was bordering on creepy given how obvious it was to anyone with a pulse that Edna worshiped Madison. Edna's problem was that she crashed right through Madison's whole idea about herself and about who she was. Madison once confessed that she had told her grade two teacher that her biggest fantasy was to grow up to be a Chandler. Little Madison wanted to grow up and to take her rightful place as a responsible member of her own family, silver fish forks and all.

At seven, I wanted to be the Green Hornet.

"Don't you think it's time?" I asked as we walked up her path. "I mean to just get it over with and tell Kit and Sarah who Edna really is? You have to know that you'll feel better getting it off your chest. And God knows she worships the dirt you drag your feet on." I couldn't see her reaction, but I could hear her sigh. "Look how well they handled the whole thing about you being adopted. That was a big so what, so I'm betting Edna will be too."

She groaned. "I know, I know, it's not even that. The woman makes me mental, and it's like if I say it out loud, say that we're related, it'll make it true for good."

"Well, yeah, it'll make denial harder for sure, but I'm just saying that it'll feel way better to get it out."

"Yeah …" she said, doubt and suspicion piercing a thousand holes in that one-syllable word.

We barely got to the door when it flew open, with Edna on the other side. Edna had a disconcerting habit of taking on "meet and greet" duties when she was over for dinner. "Come in and take a load off, girls. Fabi and me have just been yukking it up while I waited for my beautiful granddaughter."

Okay, that was suspicious. Fabiola was the real Chandler housekeeper, fiercely loved and loving in return, but a woman of few words, the Clint Eastwood of maids. "Probably pumping her for info," Madison muttered under her breath.

I jumped right in. "Hi Edna. Nice to see you again."

She somehow smiled at me without taking her eyes off Madison. "And your folks called to say they were running a bit late. Toot!"

I could feel Madison start to hyperventilate. One of Edna's unique peccadilloes was that she had serious gas issues, which made her a championship farter. At some point, Edna convinced herself that she could mask the actual farts by saying the word "toot" out loud every time she let one fly. It just about undid Madison and her father every time she did it. Her mum and her grandfather, on the other hand, found the tootings killer funny.

Edna minced over to Madison. "Look at you, doll! What a sight for sore eyes you are!"

Madison submitted to a three-second hug and then politely extricated herself. "You too, Edna. Wow, your hair … wow."

Edna's hair was another one of those peccadillo things. Today, she was sporting flame-retardant orange, which had been teased and feathered within an inch of its life. She patted her sparse but puffy puffs. "You like it? I think it's classier than the perm, toot, don't ya think?" She kept patting. "I got to keep it classy for my classy granddaughter, toot, toot!"

"I like it, Edna." Madison glared at me. Well, it *was* a step up from her most recent "do," which was a conflicted combination of tight little curls in front and straight as a plank in the back. Edna always said she didn't give a "tinker's damn" what people thought of her when she was leaving a room.

"Want a drink, kids?"

"Uh?" said Madison.

"I know my honeybun will want a Coke. I'll get you one too, Sophie." And off she toddled to the bar in the den, humming Frank Sinatra's "Strangers in the Night."

"I am going to have to kill her." Madison shook her head. "I see no other way out. I mean, make yourself right at home why don't you!"

I had to admit that Edna threatened to make the Aunties look reasonable. Maybe that was why I liked her so much. No, that wasn't it. Edna had balls. Mrs. Edna Ryder, mother of Madison's biological mother, was light years below the Chandler family food chain and that didn't faze her a bit. Every time I went over for dinner, it was like they had invented some new appliance that I had to *pretend* to know how to use. The last time it was this weird little silver blob that sat above the cutlery, a knife rest. Edna had a field day with that one. There I was tracking Mrs. Chandler with sonar precision, copying her every move, all pinched and petrified that my cover would be blown, that I wouldn't *pass*. Edna did not pretend. Edna had a blast doing colour commentary on her knife rest. "Are ya tired, dear knife? Here, have a nap, toot, toot. What a hoot! What next, I ask ya?"

I followed her into the den to help with the drinks. She didn't need any. Edna used the polished silver tongs to plop sculpted ice cubes into the crystal tumblers like she'd been born to it.

"Ice is ice, honey." It was like she could feel my astonishment. "And bourbon tastes the same in crystal as it does in a Dixie cup." She took a healthy snort and then topped up before heading back to Madison. That was Edna for you. Edna who lived in assisted housing. Edna who had plastic covers on her lampshades *and* her sofa. Edna who had a Dixie cup dispenser in her kitchen for God's sake, who delighted in the gift of her new-found granddaughter, and who didn't give a fairy fart about anything else. *That* Edna thought, no, she *knew,* that she was every bit as good as the Chandlers or anybody else in the stadium. I wanted some of that.

Maybe a religion could give it to me.

I got one! I got religion! Well, religions actually. After much serious consideration, deliberation, and flipping of coins, I decided that I was going to be a Buddhist, with a bit of Jewish, and a drop of Catholic.

It felt right. My trusty encyclopedia said that Buddhism is a pile of really old spiritual teachings that mostly revolve around the concept of inner peace and God knows I wanted some of that. A bigger plus was that they seemed like a pretty flexible lot, which was perfect because I didn't want to sweat the details. The details are why I couldn't be Catholic. Catholics had way too many details.

I made an altar by piling up Mama's stockpot on top of our *Polish to English* and *Bulgarian to English* dictionaries. I covered it all with several of Auntie Luba's crocheted doilies. I got a nice long cream candle from Madison and stuck it in a silver candleholder that had belonged to Papa's grandpa in

Poland. All in all, my altar looked quite festive, if not technically accurate. Still, I was sure that Buddha would approve;
he was all about getting rid of your suffering. Between the
melodrama of my Eastern *Europeanness* and the daily opera
that was Mama, I'd cut my teeth on suffering. Enough already.
Buddhism and me—hand in glove except for the fact that the
overall vibe was maybe a bit too blissed out. I wasn't sure I
could handle that much serenity, hence the Jewish part. Not
too much, just enough to goose all that bliss and make me feel
comfortably uncomfortable.

I explained all this to Papa on the Saturday after the funeral.
Mama was showing houses, so Papa and I were having lunch.
Just like the old days.

So normal … but not.

We were enjoying our favourite meal, Auntie Eva's bread
and our special Campbell's tomato soup, which was one can
each and only half the liquids they tell you so that it's closer
to warm ketchup than soup. Heaven. He glanced at his watch.
Papa's life of leisure was pretty well over since he had been
made president, CEO, and chief driver of Pescatore's White
Night Limousines. They had inherited two ancient Italian
drivers who were good for taking people to and from the
airport but not much else. Papa did the drives to Niagara Falls,
weddings, celebrities, and stuff like that. Today, he had a run
to pick up a guest at a downtown hotel and drive him to a jazz
club in Buffalo.

"So, you're a Buddhist Jew?"

"Yup." I nodded in between slurps. "Good soup, Papa. You
haven't lost your touch with a can opener."

"High praise indeed." He winked. "A Buddhist Jew, hmm. Just how orthodox do you intend to be?"

Yes. Well. There were choices? I knew I should have paid closer attention to the *Judaism, or the Religion of Israel* section of the encyclopedia.

"Are you going to keep kosher, for instance?"

Aha! I knew about this bit. I was the Seder kid for the Kauffman family four schools back. Every Friday, I'd turn on and off their lights, their stove, and anything electrical. The Kauffmans also had two separate kitchens and even two sets of dishes. There also was something about dairy and lobsters that sprang to mind, but I couldn't put my finger on it.

"Well, there might not be any more pork in my future, but I'm not sure about *how* kosher to take it. I don't want to piss off the Buddhists."

Papa smiled.

"I bet there's like all sorts of kosher levels."

"Well, I don't know about that, but there's orthodox, modern orthodox, conservative, and reform, and then within those there are …"

"There, the last one, the reform one. That just sounds right." Yup, I was adamant. "Reform it is."

"Wise choice." Papa got up, cleared the table, and started washing the dishes. "Why Judaism at all, if I may ask?"

"Well, thing is, Buddhists are so laid-back, which is exactly what I want, but then where do I go with the Sophieness part of me and so, presto, Jewishness!" Whoa, Papa was doing dishes? Was that AA or Auntie Eva? "I like being Jewish. It feels like me."

To his credit, he didn't laugh.

"Look, I know I don't know much about either of them, but I'm going to learn and …"

"Of course you are." He kissed my forehead. "You surprise me every single day, Sophie Kandinsky."

I watched him finish drying. "You too, Papa."

"Well, my beautiful Buddhist-Jewish-Catholic, I've got to get back to the office and make some calls before I go on a run." My God, he sounded so … I don't know, like other fathers must sound on their way to work, so *I own a briefcase*. It was weird.

Papa hugged me goodbye.

I hugged back hard.

He was amazing and solid and consistent and … it's just that there were entire minutes when I didn't recognize him. Did Mama recognize him?

As soon as the door shut, I felt claustrophobic. A run would be perfect. I'd run my ass off today and tomorrow, so that by Monday's practice, I would show dragon boy that I was in fabulous shape, that I was a basketball warrior queen, invincible, superhuman, a leader of leaders.

Not that I cared.

I slapped on a decaying pair of gym shorts and one of Papa's old sweatshirts, pulled my hair back into a massive ponytail, and even though it was almost the end of September, I grabbed my designer sunglasses for good measure. They were my lucky glasses. Mike said so. He and Auntie Luba bought them for me on their honeymoon. They stayed at The Plaza in New York City, which is beyond romantic if you can wrap your head around the fact that they're both in their forties. Anyway, while they were there, Auntie Luba bought me these amazing Dior sunglasses from an entrepreneur who was selling them from a blanket on the corner of Fifth Avenue and Fifty-seventh Street. They looked fabulous on me, even though the gold *R* fell off on the very first day. Kit called them my Dios.

It was a good decision, good to be there. The park was built over a reservoir overlooking Spadina and St. Clair avenues, so it gave you a feeling of being on top of the world. This time, I almost had the place to myself, just a couple of other joggers and dog walkers. There was a running path all around the outside perimeter of the park. I planned to do at least six cycles, which would be more than two miles. That'll show him. The colours were turning fast. They got more intense with every lap. The air was just crisp enough that I could pick up a scent of burning leaves every time I rounded the southwest corner. I felt charged, electrified, the hairs on the back of my neck raised.

Wait a min—

Was that my name?

"Sophie! Sophie, wait up!"

Someone cut the cables holding up my stomach.

Couldn't be.

I ran faster, with my heart knocking around in my chest. My internal organs were a mess.

"Sophie, wait, hold on!"

Jesus God! Damn, can a Buddhist Jew say Jesus God? Think it?

I stopped but did not turn around.

"Soph, hey, I know it's you under those glasses!"

If *she* was with him, if the baby, if the child, *his* child was, I would projectile vomit.

"Sophie!"

I stopped, inhaled, and turned around. Luke. All by himself. Gorgeous, smiling, adorable Lucas Pearson.

"Hey, you look great, Sophie." He flashed his lone dimple.

I exhaled into his smile and then fixated on the fact that I was wearing gangrenous gym shorts and a fifteen-year-old sweatshirt. In a stupendously pathetic attempt to look better I sucked in my stomach and willed my lips to turn glossy.

"It must be the Dios." He looked perplexed. "My sunglasses." I took them off.

"Nope." He shook his head. "Still great, in fact, even greater now that I can see your eyes. How are you, Sophie?" He stepped closer to me. Perilously close.

Fabulous, Holy Buddha, never better.

"Good. Okay. You know." I stuck one of the sunglass arms into my mouth and chewed on it thoughtfully. I saw Farrah Fawcett do that once on *Charlie's Angels* and all the bad guys swooned, except I stuck it too far down and gagged.

A jogger blew by us and shot me a dirty look. Luke took my elbow and led me off the path. He walked us over to a massive chestnut, my favourite tree in the whole park.

"I watched you run for a while. Hope you don't mind. Your form is impressive."

Well, we can thank your best friend, the drill sergeant, for that. But I didn't say anything because Lucas Pearson was holding my arm, hence, words were out of the question. Jesus, he still smelled of Sunlight Soap. I extricated myself before I got flooded by the physical memory of him.

It was instantly colder. I shivered. He moved to put his arm around me.

Stopped. Stepped back.

Colder still.

"Luke, were you at, did you come to Luigi's funeral?"

"Yeah, sorry." He stroked the tree trunk. I looked longingly at the tree. "I wanted to pay my respects."

I was aware that he looked haunted or hunted. I was aware that there were circles under his eyes, blue circles, blue eyes, stubble on his jaw. Luke was tired. I was also aware that all this made him more gorgeous. I scanned my word file for something to say, then remembered that it was his turn to speak. He didn't. Instead, he reached over and touched my lips with his fingers.

Jesus God Buddha Moses.

He drew them away immediately.

We both pretended it didn't happen.

"Yeah, so I remembered Luigi from Mike and Luba's wedding."

I like to think that we both paused to remember the wedding, the dancing, the fire escape, the promises.

"But then I chickened out and snuck away as soon as you finished the reading. You did great. You looked great."

Okay, enough already. "How's … uh …" I couldn't get the words out. *Alison the slut who trapped you by getting pregnant* just didn't seem appropriate.

"Fine," he said.

"Good, good." I nodded. "And so, what are you, uh, doing?"

"Well I got my GED and now I'm working full-time at my dad's place. I'll save up a bit and then my folks will help put me through college and then …"

Blah, blah, blah, blah …

I wanted to fall into him and slap him at the same time. A gust of wind blew his hair into his eyes. I could just reach up. Instead, I shivered again. "Well, I better go," I said. "Gotta run, so to speak."

"Running is good." He had not taken his eyes off me.

Danger, danger, Sophie Kandinsky. I must never ever see him again.

"Yeah, I'll be running a lot," I said. Pause. "Here, I mean." Big pause.

"Yeah, good." Luke smiled, but he looked sad. "Running's good," he repeated. "You look good, real good." Then he turned and walked away, taking the sun and all the best parts of me with him. I watched him until he disappeared over the horizon. He did not turn around.

It was innocent. Totally. I know I didn't *do* or even say anything wrong. But I still felt wrong. Luke. Damn. Thank God for my altar. As soon as I got home, I was going to pray for forgiveness to all my new religions. Let them sort out my sins. That's what they were there for. Besides, it was way too complicated for me.

Wait, did he say I looked good?

"What's up, buttercup?" Kit watched me watch myself in the mirror. I was using mascara application as an excuse to watch me. I was enthralled with me. What did *he* see when he looked at me? I don't think he saw what I saw.

"Nothing much." I shrugged.

Madison looked up from her jewellery drawers. "Sophie, you've been staring at yourself in the mirror for an hour and a half."

Oops.

"Is this like one of your new religious traditions?" She put on an armload of bangles. "Is it a Zoro thing?"

"Zoroastrianism, and I keep telling you guys that I'm for sure a Buddhist Jew, probably."

"Yeah, but still, sweetie," said Sarah, adjusting her bra straps. "You're wearing a year's worth of mascara."

I looked at my eyes and instead Luke's blue eyes burned

through and watched me. One lousy touch and I was in trouble all over again.

Kit snapped her fingers in front of my face. "You're zoning out again. Something's up, give."

The new, spiritual Sophie was not a liar. "I was thinking of Luke," I said. The partial truth is still the truth. Ask anybody.

"Ohhh …" they said.

Total sympathy.

"Why?" asked Sarah as she threw me her Love's Fresh Lemon.

"Why what?" I asked, dousing myself in lemon.

"She means, why *now*?" Kit said.

"Well," I gathered up the lie, "I don't know, here we are getting all gussied up for a party at Makeout Mansion again, and I just flashed to my first party there, remember?"

"When we found out that you'd never been felt up or even kissed before?" Kit shook her head.

"And we had to give you emergency slow-dance lessons?" said Madison.

Sarah sighed. "Wow, a thousand years ago."

"Yeah," I agreed. "And remember Ferguson Englehardt did his best to 'make me a woman'? I swear for a minute I thought I was a lesbian." Sarah and Madison snorted. "And then Luke came after me and well, and then he touched me."

"Should be a song." Kit turned away.

"We just have to find you someone new and fabulous!" gushed Sarah. "And we'll do it tonight. I can just feel it."

"You just watch what and who you're feeling, Sarah Davis," warned Madison. "We've been lucky that our reputation is still intact with all your enthusiastic feelings. We haven't been to one of Anita's parties in forever. This is a tri-high-school party, so ..."

"So our desirability quotient is on the line for Lawrence Heights, North Toronto Park, as well as Northern." I bowed as Sarah and Kit clapped.

"Oh, just behave," groaned Madison. "I'm meeting Billy there, and I'll be too busy to monitor us."

The party was raging by the time we got to Anita Shepard's, aka Makeout Mansion. Kids spilled out of the house and onto the veranda and the lawn, even though it was cold enough to see your breath. The floor pulsed to the beat of "Boogie Fever" and the hallway reeked of incense, weed, and beer. I spotted Jessica Sherman in the far corner of the hallway with two other girls from our second string. They were a stoned, giggling heap on the floor. Not their best look.

I was way too uptight to get that out of control. I barely drank at these things, just nursed a beer through the night while I nursed my party girl reputation at the same time. Weed? I didn't know how to nurse that, so no way. The Blondes just thought scrunching up your face over a boogered joint was unseemly. Each one was a devoted Southern Comfort and Seven drinker.

Anita's had the perfect party layout. To the right was the living room, where it looked like the most devoted smokers and tokers were holding court. On the left of the hallway was the front parlour, where I headed after I grabbed a beer. The Blondes went straight for the family room in the back, where they would stash their booze in the mini-fridge. The family room is where all the action took place, the dancing, the making out, although there were also other rooms for that. Anita's always had a certain darkness, a wisp of danger. Maybe it was my imagination, but it felt extra wispy tonight.

Speaking of danger, damn, David was here. I almost turned and ran right out, but then I stiffened. No sir, no way, I had every bit as much right to be here as David Walter did. He was lounging on a back window seat with two girls hanging off him. It was like something out of a cheesy James Bond movie. Not that I cared.

Then David saw me. He looked more put out than he usually did when he saw me.

I took a sip of my beer and raised it to him.

He looked even more irritated. What?! Did he hate immigrants, was it my hair, the Alison-Luke thing, what? One of the girls was nibbling his ear. I vaguely recognized her as a friend of Anita's. I thought deeply uncharitable thoughts about her until I looked away. Then I looked back, but just out of the corner of my eye so he couldn't tell I was looking. The other one—the one that wasn't chewing on his ear like it was one of the seven food groups, was rubbing his stomach. Jesus God! I mean, under his shirt, in full view of everyone. It was appalling, but it was also like a car wreck. I couldn't look away. Then Buddha, thank God, sent Sue Winger, a senior from Lawrence Park, over to me. Sue is a motor-mouth extraordinaire and she blocked my view. It was at least twenty minutes before I could extricate myself from her, and I only did that when Madison ran back for a courage hug. "What *courage hug*?" But she was off again.

I couldn't wait to tell Kit and Sarah that our assistant coach was mercilessly assaulting two girls at the same time. Where were they, anyway? They didn't usually hang out in the backroom. I started looking for them down the hall and under the stairway nook. Nope. In the front dining room. Nope. I chatted to a couple of football players in the library, including Paul Wexler, who tended to light up whenever he saw me, if I do say so myself. My beer was bathwater warm by the time I got to the family room.

Oh dear.

Kit was on top of a coffee table shaking her booty to "Shake, Shake, Shake, Shake Your Booty." Rick Metcalfe, who had never gotten over her, was alternately egging her on and trying to get her off to be with him. Now, Kit was a spirited kind of kid, but this was beyond exuberance. I searched for potential reinforcements and spotted Sarah in a corner slow dancing with George, Mike's nephew. Not only was it *not* a slow song, but Sarah was in a take-no-oxygen lip-lock with the boy.

What in Moses' name …?

I marched over and tapped Sarah on her back.

"Sophie, baby! How's it hanging, shnookums?" She giggled. Then George giggled.

Guys don't giggle. Shnookums? She swayed and smiled dreamily. "Sarah, you're wasted! How could you do that? We haven't even been here an hour." I glared at George, who grinned back at me.

"Not poshible," she slurred. "Just had the one Southern 'n' Sheven, not even."

"It's true." George could not stop giggling. "I got it for her and she hasn't had another one. We've been dancing."

"You've been groping, you mean." I looked back at the coffee table. Kit was still putting on an energetic floor show. Madison was nowhere to be found. Our platinum reputation would take a hit if these two kept going at the rate they were going. Rick was joined by Stewart Allen and Ben Wheeler in cheering on Kit. I grabbed Sarah's hand and started walking to Kit. "Help me get her off."

"Sure, shnookums. Hey, Kit!" Sarah waved at her like Kit was on the other side of the street. "Sophie thinks you gotta get your butt down, girl!"

Kit waved back and blew me a kiss.

"Need some help with your team, shnookums?" Oh get me a gun, it was David. He smiled at me. He'd never smiled at me before. Alert the press! He was amused all right. David kept smiling, even though he was bimbo free.

"No thank you, coach!" I *retorted.* I've been working on my retorts since the second practice. I just didn't think I'd be retorting at a party.

David leaned into me. "If you girls can't handle your liquor, you shouldn't be at the big boys' party. Things happen at Anita's. Go away, little girl." He leaned in even closer. "You don't belong here, Sophie."

I got a little woozy when he said my name. Then I came to. What the hell! How dare he? "First of all, *coach,* we've been to plenty of Anita's parties!" Which technically wasn't the God's honest truth. We'd only been to a couple over the years. The rumours, come to think of it, were that the parties had cranked up lately, but Madison had arranged to meet

Billy here and the rest of us were dead keen to see and be seen.

"Second of all, *coach,* I don't drink!" I waved my bottle. "I just pretend to." Why was I telling him this? Shut up, shut up! "And third, *coach,* they are *NOT* drunk. They haven't had enough time to get drunk!"

Kit chose that moment to belt out a rollicking rendition of Captain and Tennille's "Love Will Keep Us Together" mixed into the Canadian national anthem. Rick was seething with unrequited love, or something.

I had to get that girl out of here. Sarah boogied up beside me.

David grabbed my arm. "They're pissed." I swear he was growling. "Get them, and you, out of here. It gets worse. And stop calling me coach!"

I tried to wrench my arm free. "Sorry," I said, *"assistant coach!"* He gripped tighter. It felt like I was standing in front of a furnace. Thank God, I couldn't blush. "And, I keep telling you, they're not drunk! Kit, get down off that coffee table right now!"

"Shophie's right. We're shober," said Sarah just before she puked on his shoe.

It was a small barf.

More like a spit up, really.

At least it got Kit off the coffee table. She was over in one bound opening up her little party purse. "I have a Kleenex. There!" She whipped out a tampon and started dabbing his shoe with it.

Somehow I did not disintegrate. David still had me by the

arm, though more gently now. He was chewing his cheek. Papa did that too. When he was trying not to laugh.

"What in God's name!" Finally, the Mounties had arrived. Madison was here. "Why is Kit mopping up your shoe with a tampon? Did she throw up? She threw up! Are they pissed? How could they be pissed? They're pissed!" Sadly, this entire set of accusations was aimed directly at me.

David burst out laughing. I could have killed her.

"Oh yeah, well, where were you?" I demanded in a demanding type of whisper. "And it better be good." I'll show her. Two can play at this game. Why was *I* responsible for them? "Well?"

"I was breaking up with Billy on the back deck."

"Oh, right, 'courage hug.'"

David let out a long slow whistle while Kit seized this opportunity to crumple over onto the floor and stay there.

"They're drunk!" Madison threw up her hands. "And you're blushing!" Apparently, we were back to blaming me again. "I've never seen you blush!"

"I don't blush," I reminded her.

David turned me toward him. "Maybe not, little captain, but your cheeks are a very becoming shade of firehouse red." He had two clear-as-day dimples when he smiled that way. I wanted to kick him.

"I do not blush!"

"Well you do now, and they're plastered." Madison tried to lift Kit and got nowhere.

"No, no, no, no," explained Sarah.

George weaved over to us with a glass of water for Sarah.

"No guff, man." He shrugged. "I wouldn't get her loaded. All she had was one drink and we shared a brownie."

"Great brownies!" agreed Kit from the floor.

Madison, David, and I looked at one another. "Hash brownies," nodded David. "That'd do it."

Hash? Holy Moses. "Is this like permanent? Are they going to be okay?"

"Not after I kill them for being terminally stupid," said Madison.

"They'll be fine tomorrow," David sighed. "But we better get them home."

"I got my wheels." George tried to pull himself up to his full height, which was impressive, but he was still half a head below David.

David turned to him. This could turn into a pissing contest. "You're stoned, man. Chill out okay? I'll bring 'em home."

George's eyes narrowed. You could tell he didn't want to leave Sarah. George was two years older, but David didn't flinch. They stared at each other. Finally, George put his arm around a heavily listing Sarah. "I'll help you get them to the car."

"We're all staying at Madison's tonight," I offered.

"Lucky me." David winked. "One-stop shopping."

George and David somehow stuffed Sarah and Kit into the car, despite them both insisting on a slow dance out in the middle of the street. We put them on either side of Madison in the back, while I got in the front with David. Even in the dark, I could tell he found this whole episode enormously enter-taining. I tried to keep my cringing and whinging invisible,

but then they launched into a hash-brownie version of Frankie
Valli's "My Eyes Adored You." Frankie Valli struggles with
that song. It was excruciating. Even if David Walter never said
anything about tonight, about any of this, he knew, and he
knew that I knew that he knew, and he … oh never mind. It
was embarrassing, period.

They finally shut up as we pulled into Madison's circular
driveway. After much negotiation, we decided that Madison
and I would haul in Kit, while David helped Sarah. Halfway
up the walk Sarah stumbled and David swooped her up like it
was an afterthought. He just picked Sarah up and carried her
the rest of the way, including up and into the house and up all
those stairs to Madison's room. It was not something that I
was ever going to forget. He didn't even break stride. I felt my
cheeks fire up again. Thank Buddha I don't blush, no matter
what they said. Fabi came out in curlers and rescued Kit from
Madison's death grip as David trotted back out.

"Hash brownies," mouthed Madison to Fabi like it would
mean something to her.

Fabi nodded and helped Madison with Kit. Meanwhile, I
ran back to the car to retrieve our purses. David draped himself
over the car door as I reached into the back seat. "Practice is
Monday morning at 7:30 A.M. Think you can have your team
ready, *captain*?"

"No problem." I grabbed all the purses. "You can go now. I
can take it from here." Instead, he sat on the hood.

"Hmm." He shook his head. "I think I better wait until you
get in. God only knows what end of trouble you could get
yourself into between here and the doorway."

I got hot again. Maybe I was going through menopause. None of this was making sense. "It's okay, really. You can go home now."

"Home?" He crossed his arms and looked at his watch. "It's not even midnight, little girl." His voice low and smoky.

Now I was cold.

"As soon as you're safe, I'm going back to the big boys' party."

The girls, those girls at Anita's. He was revolting.

"Good night, Sophie …"

I ran up the walkway.

"You're welcome!" he called.

If we weren't at Madison's, if I wasn't freaked about waking up the whole neighbourhood, wouldn't I just slam the door, *hard*. "Thank you, David," I said through gritted teeth and without turning around.

"Why, you're welcome, Sophie." I swear I could hear his smile. I did hear his car door open and shut, and then the engine catch and go. Safely on the other side of the door, my heart thumped so hard I thought Fabi would come running.

Madison appeared at the top of the stairs. "What a night, eh?" She waved at me to hurry. "Thank God David was there."

"I suppose," I muttered, dragging my feet and thumping heart up the stairs.

"Did you see him just toss Sarah into his arms? I mean, oh my, wow!"

"Yeah, oh my," I said.

"He is like nobody else!"

I bet he was speeding, couldn't wait to get back to *them*.

"We owe him now." She folded her arms dramatically, a gesture worthy of Auntie Eva. "You have to promise to behave better around him."

"What, me? Why?"

"Because he saved our ass tonight, Sophie Kandinsky, and you know it."

David being smothered by them. Doesn't matter, didn't matter, why would I care? I didn't care. "I don't care!" I said. Madison looked momentarily confused. Apparently we were having a whole different conversation.

"Well you should! I need you to promise to behave, Sophie."

"He'll be extra unbearable now, all high and mighty, so full of himself, besides he's the one that's all snotty to me!"

"Sophie ..."

"Yeah, yeah." This was going to take some serious face time in front of my altar. I even made a sign of the cross as soon as we turned off the lights. Didn't help. I heard him whispering all night long. *Go away, little girl, go away, little girl, go away ...*

"So vat is it, buboola?" Auntie Eva was fussing with coffeecake, bread, schnitzel, kielbasa, sausages, hard-boiled eggs, and pickles. Everything you need for a quick snack. Instead of going home after spending the night at Madison's, I asked a mildly mortified Kit to drop me off at Auntie Eva's. I had to reassure her the whole way that the previous night's damage was limited, thanks to the ever-so-smug David. We did not revisit her tampon-mopping or table-hopping.

Mama had showings all day, and I just didn't want to trip around an empty condo. So, here I was at crazy Eva's. She was whipping out Royal Crown Derby teacups and Waterford crystal shot glasses. "Auntie Eva, it's just me. This is so not necessary."

"Shhht, shhht!" she said, brandishing a knife. "Iz not every day my baby buboola comes to see her Auntie Eva. It iz an occasion. *Da?*" She resumed kielbasa cutting. "Vy do you tink I put up vit your koo-koo Mama and Papa? It is only for you, because *you* are dat fantastik and beautiful!"

I defy anybody not to melt in the face of that much enthusiastic adoration.

"I love you too, Auntie Eva."

Uh-oh. Mistake. She thundered over at lightning speed, carving knife in hand, and smother-hugged me. An Auntie special where your face is shoved into voluminous bits of fabric, 72-Hour Wonderbra, and Auntie mass.

Just before I was about to pass out, she returned to the kielbasa. "So vhy are you greasing me vit your present?"

I thought about it … and then let it go. I shrugged and bit my lip. Then, "You mean, *gracing me with your presence*?" I couldn't help myself.

"*Zat* is vat I said." But her heart wasn't in it. She raised an eyebrow and sat across from me. "Are you maybe feeling a depressing coming on after all? Vas ve vrong in tinking you are not sensitive enough for a depressing?"

"I don't know." I shrugged. "What does a depression feel like?"

"If you got to ask," she smiled, "you don't got von. You are not maybe drinking too much? I know you crazy kids …"

"No, Auntie Eva, I drink my shot of brandy with you guys and that's pretty much it." We picked up our glasses, clinked to a hearty *"Živili!"*

To life.

But I was still feeling pretty lifeless, all in all.

She eyed me. "Have some kielbasa, eat. Iz not good for your breasts if you get too skinny."

"Is it made with pork?"

"*Pa* sure," she said proudly. "I got it from za Ukrainian butcher."

"Sorry, Auntie Eva, I can't eat pork. It's against one of my religions."

"But za Hindu peoples eat pork. I asked to za Indian lady next door. Cows are a problem, but not za pig."

Hindu? How did she get Hindu? "No, Auntie Eva, I'm a Buddhist Jew." But then again, Hindu might be fun. I made a note to myself to look it up as soon as I got back home.

"Oh." She looked confused. "So za Buddhist part cancels za Jewish part, no?"

"No." I shook my head. "Buddhists are vegetarian." Auntie Eva clutched her chest. I might as well have said *heroin addict*. "Although it may not be a totally strict thing." She sat down again. "And I'm going to be this reform kind of Jewish, but even they maybe have a pork thing, you see. And of course I'm a little bit Catholic too."

"Of course." She nodded. "I vill remember for fish on Fridays."

I'm not an idiot. I *know* I sounded like an idiot. Thing is, she didn't treat me like one when she could have, maybe should have. Instead Auntie Eva did her level best to keep my religions straight and not step on my spiritual toes.

"Zer vas for sure lotsa God vit za drunks, *da*?"

"Yeah," I agreed. "That's where I got the idea."

She hustled right back to the kitchen and came back wielding more meat. "Beef salami!" She looked triumphant. "It vas a good place, *da*?"

"Yeah." I nodded. "I didn't feel weird there at all."

"Yoy!" Massive chest clutching. "You are feeling veird vit your Auntie Eva?"

"No, Auntie Eva." I was smother-hugged again. "How could anyone feel weird with you?" I mumbled into her chest. She let go and examined me like she was counting freckles. "Iz not your fault, Sophie, za drinking, za prison, za separation."

"Still, it's a hell of a list when you start thinking about it." I downed my brandy and went for the beef salami.

Auntie Eva grabbed both of my arms. "I love zem boat." She looked to the ceiling. "Even sometimes your Papa. But zey are boat crazy peoples. Vat zey do iz because of Magda and Slavko not because of you. Iz *not* your fault, understand?"

"I know." I nodded. I knew I didn't make the world go around, make parents drink or break up, whatever. I *knew* that. But I also knew that there had to have been something I should have done, should be doing right now even, but didn't know what or how. "I better get back now. Mama will be home." Auntie Eva eyed me, hard. She wasn't buying it. I saw it play out underneath her makeup.

"Okay," she sighed. She was going to let it pass. After one more smother hug for the road, I was off. "Even zo it's for sure zer stupid fault," she called from the doorway, "you must cut some slacks for zem."

"You mean, cut them some slack!" I yelled from the sidewalk.

"*Zat* is vat I said!" she yelled back.

She did that one on purpose. I was still smiling when I got home.

Mama whipped open the door as I was rooting around for my key. I braced myself for the full-frontal assault. How was the party? Was there drinking? Were there drugs? What did I do? How was it at Madison's? When was I going to do my homework? What tests did I have this week? Did I have morning or afternoon practice? And on and on.

Instead she said, "Good, let's go!"

"Huh? Where?"

"To da Alcoholics' Club!" She glanced at her watch.

"What?"

"Remember, dey have da open meetings at 4 P.M.? Let's go! You vant to? Ve vill go instantly, right avay."

Auntie Eva must have called as soon as she shut the door. And said what? I wondered. "Sure." I nodded.

"Good!" She ran back into her bedroom. I plopped onto the sofa. It was 3:35, Mama's "instant" departures were usually hobbled by finding the right pair of shoes, which meant a change of skirts, which necessitated a different handbag, which meant a slow transfer of all items from one bag to the other, which meant a check to see whether the lipstick was still suitable, which of course, it never was so....

"Ready?"

Three forty-one, surely a new Mama record. She grabbed some business cards.

"Mama, not at an AA meeting!"

"I vont push," she promised. "But alcoholics need someplace to live, too."

I tossed my overnight bag into my room and joined her.

I felt all bubbly the whole way over in the car. Mama sang

"Clang, Clang, Clang Went the Trolley" from the movie *Meet Me in St. Louis* with Judy Garland. She's been turning to movie musicals a lot lately, and Judy Garland in particular. Judy was Mama's girl when she was extra fried.

Some of the men were outside smoking, like the last time. I guess the guys in the suits and pressed pants were inside. Some of the outside guys were rough and unshaven, some were missing teeth, some were missing showers. All of them smiled at us, at me.

"Hi, welcome back."

"Hey, good to see you."

"Welcome."

They missed me! I lit up and calmed down at the same time. As we made our way up the aisle, Mama whispered, "Papa and I are going out on za date on Friday."

I made my way into the row. "You can't date. You're married. Married people don't date."

People around us smiled, welcomed, smiled some more.

"I read about it in za *Good Housekeeping* magazine," she sniffed. "A date night brings back za romance and completely, totally, for sure, revitalizes za marriage."

Right. Only if Papa had read the same article. Otherwise, I was pretty sure that he'd think that he was just going out for spaghetti.

"Good evening and welcome. My name is Jake and I'm an alcoholic."

"Hi Jake," we all said. I wondered why Peter, our MC from last time, wasn't up there. I saw him in the third row. Maybe it was a rotating deal. I looked around the room, reread all the

Twelve Steps, and unwound a bit. The basement had worked its magic again. I was about to tell Mama when I noticed that she wasn't really there. Mama wasn't listening to Jake or anyone because she was so full of my father. I could tell. I knew all the signs. An almost smile, laughing eyes. She was with him. Papa might as well be sitting beside her. Mama was hearing his music, his poetry.

We went on to the Serenity Prayer. I knew it off by heart now. I had taken to praying it in front of my Buddhist-Jewish-Catholic altar every day, well almost every day. Despite that, it was like I hadn't heard the words until this minute. Mama and I stood up.

"God grant me the serenity to accept the things I cannot change. Courage to change the things I can. And the wisdom to know the difference."

She didn't even pretend to mouth the words. As soon as we sat down again, Mama grabbed my knee and whispered, "He is for sure finished vit za drinking." An elderly gentleman in front of her turned around and smiled a smile that could crack your heart.

We smiled back.

"And, after ve have some revitalizing dates," her nails dug deeper into my knee, "Papa vill move back to da home right avay. Home."

Silent sirens fired in and around me here in this most welcoming and protected of places. Who was she trying to convince? My mother was the most powerful person on earth. She brought out the sun every single day. She moved us seven times by herself to protect me. Made the trip to the Kingston

Penitentiary by herself for years. Commanded the all-powerful Aunties. Worked two jobs, scraped and scrambled until she bought us a place to live in a "good" neighbourhood. Mama could do anything … except maybe be without Papa.

Jake was introducing the speaker for tonight.

It was hard to breathe.

"I promise," she mouthed.

That word. God, I *hated* that word. A promise was a low-down lying thing. It was a movie star dressed in sequins and dirty underwear. Mama of all people should know that. Papa *promised* her as much as he *promised* me. So, here in this sacred place, full of God and drunks, it came to me clearly. I couldn't trust her. Mama was not infallible. Mama was just my mother. And even here in this sacred place, that little piece of clarity left me shivering.

We played Oakwood High our second game out. I don't know what those parents do to their kids out there at St. Clair Avenue and Dufferin Street, but they're behemoths, every single one of them, the players, the fans, everybody. A behemoth is a big Biblical-type beast. My spiritual quest was doing wonders for my vocabulary. I had to look up every other word in the religions encyclopedia. Anyway, Oakwood's senior team, hell, even their junior team, didn't have a girl on it that didn't clock in at seven feet, 250 pounds, *and* was fast. I lit two candles on my altar this morning and prayed to everybody on there. Oakwood scared the crap out of us. Our entire team, including subs, didn't add up to 250 pounds.

Oakwood won city champs last year when me and the Blondes should technically still have been on Northern's junior team. They used us for kindling on their march toward the finals. Okay, so maybe all the teams did that, but Oakwood injected an element of sadism into the march. For over a month now, David was on our butts, drilling harder, demanding greater speed, increasing shot percentage, and, this last week in particular, asking us to play dirtier. He calls it "combating, negating, and isolating" questionable plays. Word is that his father, an American, was a former Navy SEAL, which must have had something to do with our workouts. I hate to admit it, but we were better. We were also still three thousand pounds too light, and all the suicides in the world weren't going to change that.

As we warmed up, we tried to ignore them warming up. It didn't work. Just the sound of heavy feet pounding the floor as they sunk in all their practice shots was unnerving. David threw me a ball and was in front of me, guarding, in a split second. "Suck it up and shake them off, Sophie," he hissed. "Are you the captain, or do you want to fetch towels and oranges?"

I hated his guts and each one of his internal organs, kidneys, spleen … he was right.

Every time I peeked over at them lumbering through their drills, the power and snap of their passes, their sheer size, a little more of my mojo leaked out. Okay. No more. I made a quick and tiny sign of the cross, hoping that Buddha and Moses and everybody else who was holy would be okay with it, and then I deked by him and made my shot.

"I am the captain," I turned to him, "sir."

He shot me another ball. "Yes, you are, Sophie."

Would it kill him to smile?

"Yoohoo, yoohoo, Sophie!"

I knew they were coming and still it was a shock. I think I

go into hard-core denial until I'm faced with incontrovertible proof. In this case it was Mama, waving a white lace hanky at me. "Hallo, darrrling!" The Blondes waved back, knowing full well that that just encourages them. Auntie Eva, Auntie Radmila, and Auntie Luba all fished around their handbags until they found their white lace hankies. This was hampered somewhat by them trying to find good seats right behind the basket, which required displacing some Oakwood fans who were even more menacing looking than their team.

We were whistled off the floor, reviewed our strategy in the huddle, and whistled back onto the floor to start. Our *fans* were whooping and waving their little hankies in a furious show of support.

Madison jogged around me before she took her place for the jump. "Soph?" She smiled. "What's with the Kleenex?"

"Hankies," I corrected. "Papa made the fatal mistake of trying to explain 'the terrible towel' tradition that the Pittsburgh Steelers football team started last year." She looked blank. "Thousands of Pittsburgh's most loyal fans noisily wave team towels at every opportunity to throw off the opposition. Unfortunately, Auntie Eva thinks it's the most brilliant strategy in the history of sports."

"So, we have the horrible hankies?" She trotted over to centre court.

"Seems like it." Since he had to work, Papa swore that he would review all the rules and finer points of the game before he dropped them off. Easier said than done. My devoted fan base had been getting it exuberantly wrong for years. Twenty minutes of rules review wasn't going to change that.

The ref blew the whistle, we lost the toss, and my stomach rearranged itself into a gnarled knot.

"Boo, boo, yoohoo, boo, boo!" Dear Moses, was that their new cheer? Hankies waved with abandon. The Oakwood fans looked confused.

They were down our throats in an instant. "Move it or lose it, captain. Let's go!" David ran up and down the court with us on the sidelines.

Suddenly the floor charged with electricity.

I stole the ball and ran up with Kit. As soon as I snapped it to her, I glanced in the direction of the hankies, then farther up. Yes, top right, last row. The ball came back to me, over to Sarah, back to me, to Kit, fake, to me, double fake, and over to Madison for two points. We were on the board. The horrible hankies went wild. He was sitting now, trying to blend in. Luke could never blend in.

I remembered that they lived nearby. They. Did anyone else see?

Oakwood snapped a pass to their left forward. I shot through and stole it. Kit was up the court in a flash, snap to Kit, back to me, a fake to Madison, and I walked in for the layup; 4 to 2.

"*Da, da,* dat's it, baby girl!" Mama was standing and yelling now. There was no passing her off as a casual fan. "Papa said to show your balls!"

My Oakwood forward looked puzzled for a nanosecond, just long enough for me snatch the ball again. I fired it to Madison, who leapt like a gazelle over an Oakwood player, got the shot, and was hit hard on the way down. Two more points, plus the free throw. We knew lining up around the key that any element of surprise we had on them was evaporating and that it was going to be ugly from here on in. I didn't care. Luke was here and I was fearless. Kit trotted over to smack my butt when she caught me looking at the upper part of the stands.

"Damn," she said. "Stay with me, girl."

"Yay, yoohoo, yoohoo, yay, Madison, Madison, ya *da* ya!"

Not surprisingly, the horrible hankies didn't grasp the finer points of the terrible-towel tradition, like you're not supposed to distract your own players. Madison made the shot anyway. I was elbowed just tossing the loose ball back to their guard. Okay, now it begins....

I threw myself at everything and Oakwood fouled me like I was a two-for-one sale. The horrible hankies had the time of their lives. And I am ashamed to say that I posed. Luke was looking. I couldn't help myself. For every single free throw, I elongated, bounced the ball just so, pulled the ball into my chest, and then tossed it up and over, holding the follow-through just a beat or two longer than was necessary. In between bounces, I cursed the stupid dorky tunics that Northern made us wear. Oakwood had silky shorts and sleeveless jerseys. Trying to look sexy and fierce in a navy blue tunic and grey bloomers was tough, but I still posed my guts out. And it worked. I'd have to remember my posing technique in future. I made thirteen out of a possible sixteen foul point shots in the first half. Coach took me off five minutes before the half ended. I knew it was David's idea.

I looked up.

Gone.

David caught me searching. Had he seen?

He called me over, looking like I was holding his loved ones hostage instead of winning his game for him. "Sarah needs some confidence," he said, "some juice." It was true, they were double-teaming her and she only had four points. "Give it to her, captain."

What the hell? There wasn't a piece of me that wasn't in pain. I looked up again. Still gone. Never mind all those amazing posing points, he wanted more? The whistle blew and I yelled, "It's all yours, Sarah," as I ran back on court, replacing Kathy Bicks. "Let's crank it up!"

"Got it!" said Kit bringing up the ball. She snapped to me, I snapped to Madison, Madison dribbled and ducked and snapped to Sarah, who made the shot and got the foul, even though I'd have to say she had charged the Oakwood player. Since that was like throwing yourself onto a skyscraper, we noticed that the refs tended to err our way on those fouls. She made the shot. The horrible hankies levitated. Our bench went wild, the buzzer blew, and we trotted off at the half with a tie. Sarah glided off the courts. I snuck a peek at the stands.

"He left when David called you off," whispered Kit. Before I could say anything, she threw her arm around my neck. "Welcome back, captain. Haven't seen you play like that in forever!"

David threw me a towel. "You're playing like you're hungry." Pause, slight nod. "I want you hungrier in the second half."

I mean one lousy little smile. Seriously, would it kill him?

I gave him hungrier. I was going to show him and those

Oakwood Goliaths. We used their size against them. I, we, played recklessly, drawing out all possible fouls, and the refs, God bless 'em, called them. We were diving like the Italian soccer team. My right arm was shot. It didn't matter. Kit was limping and dragging her butt from one end of the court to the other. Madison had to sub out in the third quarter and couldn't go back in, and Sarah was on it. She was the centre and they could not throw her off her game. The horrible hankies were hoarse from screaming. And what the hell, they just may have made the difference.

We won 57 to 55, no overtime.

The Aunties were down like a bullet, hugging the ref, Coach Wymeran, and David. You'd think we had just won the city championship. Which in a way, maybe we did. After getting our heads handed to us in almost every single game last year, we had just beat Oakwood—a team that we were sure to face in the finals and a team that had gone out of its way to humiliate us. David high-fived everyone, while I was smothered by Mama.

"Let go, Mama!" She just rocked me tighter. "Mama!" She let go only when Auntie Eva ripped her off me and then smothered me herself. "Remember I'm not going home with you guys," I mumbled into her well-padded shoulder. "I'm sleeping over at Kit's."

"Ve know. Your Papa is outside parking in za no parking zone." Then she tackled David. The look on his face was worth every suicide David had thrown at us this season. My five-foot-two, girdled-and-gilded Auntie smothered my six-foot-four-inch, rock-solid assistant coach. "Bravo, Valter David!"

She set him free long enough to pat his cheek. "Bravo, such a coach you are being and so, so nice to look at, eh, Sophie, eh?" More cheek patting.

To stop this, I was going to have to puke my guts out enough to make Kit stand back in awe. Wait. Was he smiling? Valter David *was* smiling. He was probably just relieved to be set free again. That and he must be used to it. One of the many unbearable things about David was that he was so aware and comfortable with the nuclear effect he had on girls, women, and now, Aunties. The team started filing into the dressing room.

I turned to Mama. "Guys, we gotta …"

"Da, da, da!" Mama whipped out her hanky, which led to one last waving and cheering spree. "Congratulations, bravo, bravo!"

David and I were the only ones left in the gym. "God, I'm, uh, sorry about that, them, uh, they're like tornadoes. Truth is, I like to think I can control them, but I can't, not even a teeny bit."

David opened the door to the dressing room still smiling. I mean, right at me, both dimples blazing. For a second my world opened.

"Congratulations, captain. That was leadership *and* fine ball."

Oh. Right. Yeah. The game. I finally had his respect as a basketball player. Great. Really. It was what I had wanted all these weeks. David winked and stepped toward me, placing his hand on the small of my back. *"Bravo,* Sophie," he whispered. Then he gently pushed me through the door. Did his hand linger on the small of my back? No, I'm sure it didn't. But my back burned even while I showered, and it burned all the way over to Kit's. I swear I felt the press of his hand for the rest of the night, and I swear it helped.

13

I've had a million sleepovers with the Blondes since grade nine, and every single one of them turned out great. Every single one. And for every single sleepover, including going over to Kit's tonight, I vibrate with anxiety. I know it all goes back to grade six and my first almost-sleepover. Mama had to come and rescue me at four in the morning. After an ever-escalating evening of humiliating the "murderer's kid," we played hide-and-go-seek. I hid in the closet. No one came to seek. I heard them laughing, eating pizza, talking … about me. I was there for over three hours before I tiptoed, terrified, into a pitch-black hallway and called Mama. That was five years ago, and I was still on high alert for any fresh disgrace.

Isn't there an expiry date for this level of dread?

The Blonde modus operandi, no matter where we were, was to lay in a ton of junk food and haul over all of our manicure/ pedicure machinery. We usually had sleepovers at Madison's, since her room was the size of our condo and Fabi kept the junk food stocked to ultimate levels, but we also had them at my place, Sarah's, and Kit's. I'd just never had a one-on-one sleepover at Kit's.

I responded with championship house-guest angst. Sleepover stress had morphed into house-guest horror. I reviewed my sleepover etiquette, my mantra. I must strive to be easygoing but not a wuss. Funny-edgy but not biting. Complimentary but not NutraSweet. Quick to laugh but not idiotic. And finally, helpful and adorable to the parents/ siblings/servants but not cloying. I had to be vigilant about all of these since I was the only one who didn't drink. I totally understood *them* drinking; how else do you survive a sleepover? I got pissed at Papa all over again for depriving me of a necessary rite of passage.

And all of that was just while you were awake, for God's sake! What if you snored, scratched your butt, or farted while you were asleep? What then? You can't stay awake all night. Believe me I've tried. I twitched all the way to Kit's.

"Hey!" called Mr. Cormier. "How's my favourite right guard?" Mr. Cormier was a dentist, although I could never really picture him doing needles and drills, especially since he was wearing an apron. "So, how did it go, ladies?"

"Great! We won, Mr. Cormier."

"It was never in doubt!" He wiped his hands on his apron. Well, I'm sure it was actually Mrs. Cormier's apron, but since she took off before I arrived on the scene, it looked entirely proper on Kit's dad. "Never in doubt!"

Kit groaned quietly. I understood quiet groaning. Mr. Cormier knew even less about basketball than the Aunties did. I once pointed out that her brothers played hockey. "So?" she said. "He learned about hockey for them. Why can't he learn about basketball for me? I mean, your mom comes all the time and she knows squat about the game. No offence."

"None taken," I assured her. "Thing is, he's got this big important job, two kids in university, a daughter at home, and meals to ruin. No offence."

"None taken," she assured me.

"And he's doing it by himself. The guy's tired. Mama would be too, if she was a regular human, plus I'm her only kid."

"Come over to the counter, ladies," he called. "I'll explain dinner." More quiet groaning. "That's beef stew in the Crock-Pot. I have late rounds at the Free Clinic, and I'll grab a sandwich there, but I'm sure the stew will be great!" We all looked at this massive white thing with a lid that was sitting in the middle of their kitchen counter.

"Brace yourself, Soph. We've exploded one lamb and one pork stew so far. We're working our way through the protein group. The cleaning lady went ballistic."

"Nonsense!" Mr. Cormier patted the machine gingerly. "It's the cleaning lady's recipe this time. It'll buzz or clang or something when it's done," he looked at his watch, "in ten minutes or so." Then he adjusted his tie and slipped on his jacket.

"A jacket *and* a tie, Dad? For the Free Clinic?"

Mr. Cormier's ears reddened. The man was stupendously out of his element when it came to his daughter, but that never stopped him. Maybe he couldn't come to our games, but he always tried to buy the right tampons and the perfect leg-shaving cream and even ventured into dangerous Crock-Pot recipes. "I'll be meeting one of my, uh, colleagues." He started for the door.

"I smell date," whispered Kit.

"I heard that! Ten minutes, girls." And the front door shut.

"Okey-doke!" Kit clapped her hands. "Let's grab a dinner plate and we can put it in front of us for protection."

BRRRRRRRING!!!

Even waiting for it, I was startled by the noise. We approached the beast warily. Kit went for the lid while I kept my plate in front of my face.

"Damn, he did it!" She shook her head, stunned. The warm and sweet aroma of the stew invaded the kitchen. "Wow, he pulled it off. Who knew?" She ladled three big dollops onto my plate.

"Kit, don't you think that, maybe, it's time to 'cut him some slacks' as Auntie Eva would say?"

"Nope, he owes me." I must have looked shocked because I was. "It's his fault she left."

Wow. She couldn't believe that. No normal breathing, human-type woman would leave *her children,* leave the country, to go and "find herself" unless she was married to a mass murderer. The topic of Mrs. Cormier got the Aunties going for outraged hours on end. And, on this one lonely point, I agreed.

"Kit, how about it was *her* decision to go? That maybe she was thinking more about herself than you guys?" Well, so much for House-Guest Rules number one through twenty-seven.

Kit sat down and tried out the stew. "Pretty good!" She took a bigger mouthful. "You always blame the woman, Sophie."

"Do not!" I said, stunned and offended at the same time.

"Yeah, you do."

I tried the stew. It was almost as good as goulash. "Nooo!"

She grabbed our plates for seconds even though I had just had a couple of bites from my firsts. "Sophie," Kit plopped on more stew, "you blamed your mom for your father's drinking *and* for him leaving."

We sat side by side on the stools at her kitchen counter.

"Well, yeah, but the thing is …"

"And … you blame Alison Hoover for—"

"Oh my God, Kit, she got herself pregnant!"

"Oh my God, Sophie," she parroted. "Do you think Luke had anything to do with that?"

I blew on the stew to cool it and me down. "Touché."

"You told me last year that your mom *made* your dad drink, remember?"

Okay, so, I may have *thought* that for a minute, *last year*.

"I don't think anyone *makes* someone drink, not your mom, not you." Kit looked up at the ceiling. "And maybe I'd rather blame my dad about Mom taking off 'cause it's easier than blaming me."

"You?"

"She waited until my brothers finished high school, but she didn't, couldn't, wait until I was through."

"That's seriously nuts, Kit. You don't really—"

She held up her hand. "Yeah, I know that now, most of the time." We cleared up and then examined the fridge for dessert options. Kit grabbed a gallon of Neapolitan ice cream for herself and I embraced a gallon of chocolate fudge. She snapped off both lids and offered me a tablespoon. It was quiet for a minute as we let the ice cream work its magic. "Thing is, she wants me to go to California and do my senior year there."

I was so stoked about having an entire gallon of ice cream to myself that I almost missed that. "What?!"

"Before we get to that 'what,' there's something else." She got up again. Put her spoon down. This was serious, Kit was walking *away* from the ice cream. "It's heavy." Kit started pacing. She was scaring me. The whole conversation had been scary, strange, off. Hell, Kit had been strange, okay, *stranger* lately.

I examined her while she paced. Perfect, skinnyish, blonde, beautiful. She was dying.

"I need a drink. Want a drink?"

I shook my head.

Ohmygodohmygod! I could hear her reach for the glass in the library bar, the tinkle of the ice cubes, the glugging of the Southern Comfort. She *promised* that she hadn't puked in over a year. Jesus, Moses, Buddha, I hated that word.

Kit came back with her drink and took a swig. She was dying of the puking disease. I should have said something sooner, earlier, before now. It was all my fault. I am gutless.

"Shit, Sophie, you look worse than I feel. Take a snort."

I took a gulp and gagged. "Too sweet."

"Easy, buttercup." She patted my back.

"Are you dying?" I asked as soon as I could get words out.

"No, you moron." She handed me back my tablespoon and

shoved the chocolate fudge down to my end of the counter. "But you'll think it's worse."

I wanted to slug her. "You have a venereal disease?"

"I'm a virgin, remember?"

Right. "Then what? Tell me!" I got up and grabbed her. "Nothing's worse than the pictures in my head! I suck at suspense! I can't take the anxiety, Kit! What?"

"Okay! I'm a … thing is … I'm, well, I'm pretty sure that I'm …"

"WHAT?" I shook her.

"A lesbian, I think, a bit, maybe, I mean probably. No, I'm sure. I think."

I let go of her. "Is this like a test or something?"

She shook her head. Oh my God, oh my God, oh my God! My thoughts were thumping and my heart was racing, or the other way around.

Kit drained her glass and plonked it onto the counter. "I need to know *exactly* what you're thinking."

Thinking? I did what I do best—worry, worry, obsess, and fret. In a nanosecond I did the tour. It was like the stations of the cross. I worried about Kit, her father, her mother, the Blondes, and then Kit some more, but God help me, mainly, I worried about me. What did this all mean for *me*? How was it going to affect *me*? And oh, sweet Buddha, did she have a crush on *me*? Help. Help.

Obviously, I couldn't tell Kit that. Tears pooled in her eyes waiting for a release signal.

"Breathe, Sophie. What *are* you thinking?!"

"Well, I'm trying to think what Buddha would do?"

"What the hell?"

"Or Moses or Gandhi."

"Okay, I'm pretty sure the last guy isn't a religion and that you're nuts."

"Yeah." I smiled. "Breathe, Kit."

She smiled back.

"Are you sure? How can you be sure? I mean you spelled out Rick Metcalfe's name in hickeys on his stomach for God's sake! It could be a phase, or lots of people talk about being, um, I think it's bisexual, which means ..."

"I know what it means, Sophie."

I followed her down to the rec room not even feeling my legs. "I know what it means because I've been seeing shrinks for two years, remember? Two years, Sophie. I've been exploring the crap out of this. I am what I am." She plopped down on a beanbag chair. I plopped on the one opposite her. "It's why my mom wants me to go to California with her. She says it'll be easier all around."

"Your dad?"

She shook her head. "Not yet."

We sat there. Lesbian, she thinks she's a lesbian.

"Say something, Sophie."

"Ohmygod, ohmygod, ohmygod."

Kit groaned.

"Okay, *oy vey!*"

That stopped her in her tracks. "*Oy vey,* Sophie? Seriously?"

"What? It's a Biblical Hebrew thing and hence it is an exclamation that is entirely in keeping with one of my faiths."

"You're stalling."

"Yes."

"What do you really want to ask?"

"Nothing, it's just that, well, lesbians *and* California, it's too much, too many big things to process, these big things, I mean." She folded her arms. "Okay, have you ever, uh, well have you …"

"Made out with a girl?"

I nodded.

"No."

"Then how do you know? See, that's my point, you—"

"I *know*. One *knows* these things. It's the laws of attraction. I tried to make myself like Rick or any guy. I *tried,* Sophie, I tried really, really hard."

My heart was going to break out of my chest, but I nodded my most calm and understanding nod. "Well, thing is, I've got to be wondering, just a bit, not a lot mind you, but like, have you ever been, well, attracted to, well for instance, someone like me?"

"Someone *like* you or you, Soph?" She snorted. "Relax, you're adorable, and I can see why the guys like you, but no, you're not my type."

I didn't know whether to be insulted or relieved. I was leaning toward insulted when she jumped up to go upstairs and get another drink. "How about Madison?" I asked.

"Yeah, way back in middle school." She loped up the stairs and loped back down a moment later with drink in hand.

"Well, everyone has a crush on Madison for God's sake, that's why she's Madison. That just proves it!" I insisted. "It *is* a phase. You read about this kind of thing all the time in novels about the British boarding school system. The girls all make out together while they're studying for their A levels. Just because you weren't attracted to Rick in the end …"

"But I was *attracted* to a player on the Jarvis team last year, and one on Lawrence's this year, and then my female shrink in California, and then …"

"Okay, stop. I get it."

"No, you don't." She kneeled. "I can't help it, Sophie. It's the way your God made me. The burn you felt when Luke touched you?"

I nodded.

"A guy can't do that for me. It's a lot … I know. I've been practising telling you all summer and all of September. Can you live with, with it?"

Live with it? Me? My fret cycle went into overdrive. Well, yeah, I suppose, if I have to, if she can't switch back I mean. Jesus God. I was going to have to check it out in the *Living Faiths Encyclopaedia*. I may have to change religions again and find one that will accommodate one of your best friends being a lesbian. And I knew I wasn't going to get any sleep tonight no matter what she said about me not being her type. And, of course, this was going to have to be a secret. What a whopper! How much would I have to lie? How was I going to keep a straight face when we all talked about guys? If I couldn't stand all the not knowing, how could she? What does it feel like? What would happen when she told? And there was no way I was going to let her run off to California. Her family, her life, her friends were here, right here.

I came up for air. "You gotta give me some time, okay?"

"Sure, cool." Her eyes welled up again.

"So how does it work, exactly? What goes where?"

She unwelled and heaved a pillow at me.

"Hey! I am merely trying to be sensitive and supportive here."

"And nosy!" She threw another pillow. "Your guess is as good as mine!"

I opened a bag of salt and vinegar chips. "So, let's speculate." I also opened up a family pack of Maltesers. "We'll compare notes on everything we know so far, paltry though that may be."

"It'd be better if we had Sarah here," she said. "The two of us have a pretty pitiful roster of sexual experience."

"We'll be okay. Remember, I read three hundred romance novels last year—there's not a thing I don't know." I threw both pillows back at her.

Four hours later, Kit hit the lights and was out in minutes. I watched her sleep for almost two hours, and five hours later, I went upstairs to start the coffee. I felt good. Great even. Especially considering that I had just pulled my very first all-nighter.

14

As soon as I got home from Kit's, I pulled out my trusty encyclopedia and scrolled through the relevant sections about Buddhism and Jewishness. I did not reread *Christianity: The Catholic Church Since the Reformation* because, well, for one thing, it was the smallest piece of my religious practice, so to speak, and, for the other, I was worried about what it might say.

Okay. I slammed the book shut. Okay! According to my exhaustive search, Kit was wrong. Being a lesbian wasn't this big, burn-at-the-stake thing with religions! Well, maybe in some weirdo church-type places, or maybe a thousand years ago, but not in my index. According to *The Concise Encyclopaedia of Living Faiths,* it was nothing. "Lesbian" wasn't there as a good thing or a bad thing; it just wasn't in the index at all. Therefore, being a lesbian must be a neutral "who cares" kind of thing.

Works for me.

I offered up a short but intense prayer of thanks on behalf of Kit and myself. My altar was coming along nicely. I now had a red silk runner complete with shiny tassels and embroidered gold elephants. Auntie Radmila had given me a pewter rosary, which she had had blessed in Rome, and it lived peacefully beside the small bronze Star of David that Auntie Luba found kicking around in her trunk. Finally, I had these Buddhist-type incense thingies that smelled like burnt oregano. So, I lit my candle and incense cone, made the sign of the cross, and touched the bronze Star of David. It would be okay. Kit would be okay. Please, please, please, make it okay.

Thank you, thank you. Amen.

I blew out the candle. Now what? I went to the kitchen, then the living room, then back to the kitchen again. Since it was still early in the afternoon, I assumed that Mama was showing a house. And then I remembered. It was the last Saturday in the month. Memories erupted. It had been months. I just fell out of the habit of going. The last Saturday of every month was a big glamour beauty day for the Aunties. Cast in stone, sacrosanct, and sacred. When I was little, they made me feel like the magician's assistant for their elaborate and convoluted rituals.

I jogged all the way to Auntie Eva's. Damn, I *was* in good shape.

"Hi guys!" Everyone and everything was already assembled in the dining room. "It's me! I'm here to help."

Shocked squeals, hoots, and riotous table thumping greeted me. "Sophie, buboola, baby!" fluttered Auntie Eva. They all wore their beauty uniforms, floral housedresses covered by shower curtains jerry-rigged to look like salon smocks. Auntie Radmila had on my Bambi shower curtain from three moves ago. The dining room table was pulled out to its full "seats twelve" size, and it, in turn, was covered with more shower curtains, newspapers, mud masks, toners, peroxide, creams, a dozen tweezers, lotions, and four separate piles of hair-dying accoutrements. The bowls were plopped on top of photos of near-naked Sunshine Girls that the Aunties seemed thankfully oblivious of. Added to these impressive piles were packages of Rothmans and du Maurier cigarettes, as well as seven ashtrays, Tylenol, breath mints, Courvoisier, and shot glasses.

"I svear on all my pieces, za child has grown! Little Sophie, Auntie Eva's little flower, za treasure in my chest," she sighed.

"She iz a rose in za vinter!" agreed Auntie Radmila.

Mama sat silent but beaming.

"I thought you could use my help?" I grabbed a pair of plastic gloves, snapped, pulled the fingers, and then put 'em on like I'd just done it last week.

"Sophie, are you stuffing your brassiere vit za Kleenex?" asked Auntie Radmila. Four pairs of eyes zoomed in on my boobs. I looked down.

"No, Auntie Radmila, this stunning set of 32Bs are all me."

"Hmmph!" Auntie Eva snorted. "Zey are a big B."

"Much better!" Auntie Radmila nodded in approval. You'd think she had grown them herself. "How your basketball iz doing?"

"Great, brilliant, in fact! As you know we're undefeated. In fact, we're on track for facing Oakwood at the finals." I would have gone on, gone into more details, but it would have been useless. I'd lost her. Both her and Auntie Eva were back to staring at my chest.

Auntie Eva suddenly slapped the table. "Brandy for every-bodies, you too, Magda. Don't make a face! Sophie, pour. Zis iz a celebration. Our Sophie iz back!" I poured while they rifled through their hair dye boxes.

The Aunties refused to feel stifled by a single colour or, indeed, company. Miss Clairol coexisted with L'Oréal on their heads. Auntie Eva had me mix up a combo of Champagne Blonde, Medium Blonde number 420, and Ultra Bleach Blonde, all by different companies. Auntie Radmila and Auntie Luba were similarly creative. Sometimes they mixed the dregs of all the dyes and made a soup out of it before plopping it onto their hair. Waiting to see how the colour would turn out was both nerve-racking and thrilling.

When I was little, I made meticulous notes about the names, numbers, and proportions from each mysterious box. I earnestly transcribed that information into my Hilroy notebooks, the ones with the really wide spacing. The Aunties always made a fuss about how critical this precise recording was. I was the very key to Auntie fabulousity. Of course, they never actually paid any attention to the notebooks and winged it with whatever colours they'd picked up on sale.

The ammonia bit into my nostrils and brought tears to my eyes. All was right with the world. Glasses full, we clinked to a heartier than usual *"Živili!"* Since Mama was the only one who stuck to one colour, Miss Clairol's Raven, just to touch up the grey, not that anyone would ever use that word, *grey* I mean, she was free to proceed with the face-steaming portion of the glamour treatment. Mama was shockingly low-maintenance in this crowd.

Auntie Eva rounded up all my old notebooks and a brand-new apron, which proclaimed that I was "King of the BBQ!" I mixed, stirred, and recorded like an old pro, navigating piles of peroxides, containers, bowls, and brushes, plus four separate kitchen timers.

"So, little Sophie," said Auntie Radmila, "vat iz za problem?"

She caught me off guard. "No problem." They examined me closer, concern tattooed across their faces. Mama looked guilty. Was there something she had missed? Did she drop the ball on her baby? "Really," I insisted.

"You are not sad?" Auntie Radmila persisted.

"Sad? No, I'm not sad." Trust the Croatian to sniff out sadness. Her eyes narrowed. "I'm just moody." I shrugged. "What do you want, Auntie Radmila?" I picked up my pen. Auntie Radmila thrived on complexity. "I vill do one-quarter of za dregs of vat is left from Eva's soup, mixed in vit half of Honey Blonde." She held up a Miss Clairol box marked down sixty percent and made a face. "Only one-third of za 419 and two-thirds of the Platinum Bombshell." The math alone was breathtaking.

I squirted and stirred.

Auntie Luba gave me her order in between complaining that I looked too skinny. Auntie Eva agreed while snuffing out her cigarette.

"What? We've all agreed my chest is better."

"*Da,*" nodded Auntie Luba. "Za breasts are good, but you got to find bigger hips. Zey like to have something to hang on to." Mama shoved her head deeper into the steaming bowl.

"Da!" Vigorous nodding all around.

Hmm. Alison Hoover was very curvy and so were those two barely functioning girls that were hanging off David at the party. "Hips?" I said.

"Da!" agreed Auntie Eva. She put her hands in front of her and looked at me. "Like zis."

"Phooey, Eva, too big!" Auntie Luba measured out her hands. "Your mama vas like zis."

"Leave da child alone," Mama muttered from her bowl.

"Come on, guys, that's worse than trying to grow boobs. How do I get hips, for God's sake?" I dabbed Auntie Radmila's centre part.

Auntie Eva lit up yet another cigarette. "You must for sure to stop za jogging. First it is bad for za boobies. Zey fall down ven zey get tired and zen zey stay down. You can't blame zem. And jogging jogs avay za hips!"

I dabbed poor Auntie Radmila with increasing vigour. "But I have to be in shape for basketball, or David will not respect me as captain!" They all looked at one another. Mama sighed under her towel.

"What?"

"Sophie, darrrling …" Auntie Luba patted my hand. "If you had some hips, I guarantee he vould really respect you." She winked.

Auntie Radmila nodded.

"Don't nod while I'm dabbing," I warned her. "I don't want his respect! He makes me sick, he's so stuck up and smug and …"

"Such a very unbelievable good-looking boy," nodded Auntie Eva, who was having another conversation entirely.

I finished Auntie Radmila's section, put the timer on for twenty minutes, and toddled off to Auntie Luba's centre part. "I vas stirring already," she said, all proud of herself.

"So, Sophie, ve must make you to be happy," said Auntie Eva. Auntie Luba nodded. Auntie Luba was even a more vigorous nodder than Auntie Radmila. "Don't do that," I whispered.

"Za child needs to be vorshipped by a good-looking boy." Auntie Eva winked at Auntie Radmila, Mama groaned, and Auntie Luba nodded.

I pretended I didn't hear. "Auntie Luba, quit nodding already, I'm going to end up dying your forehead!"

"Okay," she nodded. "You need za correct situation. Za basketball practice is too difficult. Ver did Madison meet her boyfriend, za lousy kisser von she got rid of?"

What can I say? They had tortured me for details.

"Uh, at her Sweet Sixteen." I finished dabbing Auntie Luba and set her timer for fifteen minutes. "Remember? I told you guys, one of her cousins brought him over from Lawrence Heights."

Mama's head popped up. "Vat Sveet Sixteen? Vat iz a Sveet Sixteen? You said she met him at her birtday party."

I reached for Auntie Eva's concoction. "Yeah, but because it was her sixteenth birthday party, it's a bigger, flashier bash, you know?"

Auntie Eva poured out more shots. They looked grim all of a sudden, well, as grim as you can look with your hair spiky with goop and your face covered in a mud mask.

"What?"

"Did Kit and Sarah also too have zis Sveet Sixteen?" asked Auntie Luba.

"Well, yeah." I shrugged. "It's the done thing, but it's just a bigger-deal birthday party, more people, more food, you know?"

They looked at one another. Mama and Auntie Luba teared up.

"What, what?"

"Ve did not make you dis Sveet Sixteen!" Mama hit her chest with her fist.

Auntie Eva got up and smothered me. "Sorry, sorry, sorry!" she wailed. I now had hair dye and clay mask on my BBQ King.

"It's okay, guys, honest. My sixteenth was last February, remember? I mean holy hell, Papa left, Luke got married, the last thing in the world I wanted was a Sweet Sixteen!"

That did it. They started blubbering and making a mess of their masks. Auntie Radmila's timer went off. "Stop crying!" I demanded. "I have to comb you through. Look guys, it's not important. It's like a class thing." They looked perplexed. "You know, for rich people, Blondes, people like that?" When will I learn?

Auntie Eva stood up again and slapped the table. "Nobody has more classes zen our Sophie!"

"Pa da!" nodded Auntie Radmila and Auntie Luba in unison.

"Stop nodding!" I yelled.

"We vill make for you a big, big party for zis year," said Mama, slowly coming to. "It vill be very completely flashy splashy vit flowers and dancing and vatever you vant!"

"Da!" Auntie Luba clapped her hands. "A Sveet Seventeen party!" This was greeted with clapping and monumental table thumping.

Oh, dear Buddha, why oh why did I open my mouth? They launched themselves headfirst into command and control party mode. It was going to be like Auntie Luba's wedding all over again. Within seconds, they decided to clear out the restaurant and have it at Mike's. It was like being carried away by a tidal wave. I gave up without a fight.

I didn't have the guts.

I looked at them, my people, my family, all hair-gooped, mud-masked, smoking, clinking shot glasses, covered in plastic shower curtains, and plotting a party for me that would be the best Northern had ever seen. Or they'd die trying.

Or I would just die.

With the Aunties, it could go either way.

15

I waited for Papa in the park. We used to come to this park even when we didn't live in the neighbourhood. We'd take the streetcar and subway to get here. It was *our* place. He was bringing coffee. Even though Papa was chronically late, I still came half an hour early. Mama was all over me, and I wasn't up for it. Guilty conscience. Mama felt like she'd dropped the ball on the whole Sweet Sixteen thing, and now in some strange punitive universe, I was being made to pay. So now Mama was all over me, examining my work, listening in on my calls, trying to unearth what else she'd missed. And then Papa called. My saviour.

The afternoon was aggressively perfect, bright and crisp around the edges. It was like a few Indian summer days got lost and then decided to stay to kiss the end of November. I shivered.

"Sophie?"

Jesus God. I turned around. I didn't dare hope to see him again, ever. Not really. I mean, what were the odds?

"Fancy meeting you here, pretty girl." He carried two cups of coffee. "Double-double, right?" One eyebrow raised, big smile.

Breathe, Sophie, breathe. Luke looked at me like no one else existed. And I believed him. He stood over me blocking the sun and radiating heat at the same time. "Double-double?" he asked again.

"Huh?" I said sweetly.

"I brought coffee."

Damn. Luke Pearson had watched me pour and drink coffee for two years at Mike's restaurant. And for two years I drank my Canadian coffee the way I drank my Turkish coffee, black with a pound of sugar.

"Double-double's great," I said. "Thanks."

Coffee moved from his hand to mine, innocently. He smiled again, one dimple showing this time. We walked over to a bench in the middle of the park. Then we sat down. Neither of us said anything. I couldn't; it was taking all I had just to inhale and exhale.

"I've been coming every Sunday since the last time," he said, finally breaking the silence. "I can't tell you how many times I've downed two double-doubles and cursed you for not showing."

Exhale.

"I made some new friends though." Luke raised his cup to three old guys sitting on a picnic bench while they watched their dogs run around in the leaves. They raised their cups back.

"I'm glad that your world is expanding," I said.

"Exploding." He tried to smile, couldn't. "But it's great to see you, Sophie, so great." He took a swig of coffee like it was whisky.

We were just sitting. Why did I feel the way I felt? So guilty, I mean. It was like I was on this big Ferris wheel of guilt and we were rounding our way back to the top. Just two people sitting on a bench … "Luke, I …" I what? I wondered. I would like to breathe? I would like my body to stop thumping? "You were at the game, our first game against Oakwood." He nodded and looked hard at the dirt.

"Hey, we made it to finals. They're this Thursday!"

He nodded.

"Oakwood." I nodded.

"Who else." He nodded.

I didn't ask him to come. He didn't volunteer. I stopped nodding.

Luke leaned forward, resting his arms on his knees, holding his cup with both hands. "It was always you, Sophie."

His back muscles twitched in and around his shoulder blades. I could touch, no, I could lay my head on his back, rest myself for a minute on Luke. And then I would be stronger and clearer … and then, oh my God, I did!

I felt him contract and then freeze in that way you do when you spy a butterfly and you don't want to scare it off. I just lay my head on the flat part of his back like it was something we did all the time. So harmless.

But not.

Was this adultery? I'd have to look up adultery in the

Encyclopaedia index. The phrase "carnal knowledge" came to mind, but I wasn't exactly sure what that meant. My hunch was that unlike lesbianism, adultery might actually turn up in the index. I knew for sure the Catholics had stuff about it, and come to think about it, it was Moses—a Jew—who wrote that stuff down.

Luke sighed and reached over to touch my thigh. I could give up the Catholic and Jewish bits.

"I can't stop thinking about you." Luke examined his coffee cup again. "My life, well my life …"

I stopped breathing. Jesus, God, *don't* talk about Alison and the baby!

"I made a mess of my life, and it's right that I should pay. Aargh!" He ran his hands through his hair. "So I come every Sunday, just 'cause maybe I could see you and pretend." I lifted my head, suddenly afraid. Luke turned and touched my cheek.

I wouldn't be the adulterer, right? Wouldn't it just be him? I'm not the married one after all. It would all be on his head. Right?

Luke leaned into me. His lips close to my face, scanning it. I could almost taste him. "If we could only, if I could only see you again, somewhere."

He smelled like a bowl of cream and I wanted to … "Papa!"

"Where?" He jerked around, panicked.

"No, I mean, I'm meeting him. He'll be here in a minute. You better go." My heart was banging around my chest. Was that excitement or panic?

Or shame?

Luke grabbed my thighs. "Tell me you'll see me again, or I won't go."

I scanned the park for Papa.

"Tell me or I won't be able to go back."

I put my coffee cup into his hand. "Yes, now go!"

"When?"

"Now!"

"No, I mean when will you meet me?"

I couldn't hear myself think with all that thrashing going on in me. "Next week. No. That's the Christmas cookie exchange thingy. The second Sunday in December, I'll come back here." Was that Papa coming up the rise? "Go, go!"

"I'll be here, next week too, just in case," he called as he jogged off. I watched him descend down the slope and then Papa ascend up the opposite slope. It was like God orchestrated it. Funny, they walked alike, long, strong strides. They were about the same height and build too. Of course, Luke was dark and Papa was fair, or else it would be seriously creepy. I felt sick and spinny. Maybe I'm not cut out to be an adulterer.

"Princessa!" Papa smiled. "How's my girl?" He folded me into him while holding onto a bag containing two more coffees. I calmed down in his hug.

"Okay. How are you, Papa?"

"Better now." He kissed the top of my head. "Now that I can see my girl."

"Yeah, I'm better now too." I opened the bag. "Coffee?"

"Two large ones!" he smiled.

"Oh boy!" I had to pee already. "Black?" I asked. All last year, Papa kept forgetting that I liked to be called Sophie rather than Sophia. Even now, he forgot sometimes, so I wasn't holding out much hope on the coffee front.

"Black of course! And no sugar."

Damn! Can nobody get that one little thing right?

"Because I brought six little packets. I know my sweetie likes it sweet, but I didn't know exactly how sweet. You can put it in, but you can't take it out, right?"

"Right!" My heart soared. "How's it going with Auntie Eva and the business?"

"The business is amazing." He glanced at his watch. "In fact, I'm sorry, but I'm going to have to leave in a few minutes. We got a last-minute call. Even adding two new drivers, we're still short all the time. I may have to buy a new stretch."

I whistled. "Wow, Papa!"

He threw his arm around my neck and kissed the top of my head. "I know, I know."

"And Auntie Eva?"

"Ha!" Papa snorted. "Not so different from Mama. She watches me like a hawk. It's actually easier being under Eva's microscope, oddly enough."

"I think I know what you mean."

We sat down. Papa leaned forward and rested his arms on his knees. Déjà vu all over again. "She asks me every day if this is the day I'm going to jump off the bandwagon. Sometimes I think I stay sober just to annoy her." He gulped down the rest of his coffee. "And then, I think she knows it and counts on it, the old biddy. They are wily creatures, your Aunties."

"It's a good thing to keep in mind," I agreed. I couldn't get over it. I mean, they sat the same way? Was it a guy thing?

"And if things get shaky, I just go to a meeting." He turned his head toward me and winked. "I go to a lot of meetings, AA meetings."

"AA meetings," I repeated. "I'm glad you've got that, somewhere to, well, somewhere to be. I get it, Papa."

For a second, he looked so sad I thought I would break. "Of course you do." He crushed the empty coffee cup. "But it's good, it's all good." He turned toward me. "I *will* make amends, Sophie. It's not a promise. I've broken too many of those." He looked at his watch again. "It's ..." He smiled at the naked trees. "It's a goal, to make you proud. That would be everything to me."

"Papa, I already am so, so proud."

"Shhh ..." Papa brought a finger to his lips. "I don't deserve it. Yet." He straightened up. "Fathers and their daughters." He looked broken and mending at the same time. What was going on?

"I pray." He shook his head. "Yes, you heard right, I *pray* I haven't caused you irreparable harm." He kissed my forehead. "Such heavy conversation for having a coffee with your old man, eh? Hey, it's not your job to figure it out, Sophie." He stood up. "Just know, I'm trying Sophia, I'm trying, and I'll do it for you. I've got to go. Walk me to the car."

We strolled arm in arm through our park, down the slope, and over to the car, serenaded the whole way by the last moments of Indian summer. My head was reeling. There was so much guilt in the pretty autumn air. Mine was understandable. I was practically a shameless adulterer on the road to hell in three different religions. But Papa, despite his big smiles—my father, who was finally getting sober, working, and clearly figuring out his life—Papa was blanketed in a guilt so thick it could warm up the whole park.

Wait a minute.

He said he was getting sober *for me,* which was brilliant except, what about for him? What about for Mama? More importantly, what if "for me" wasn't enough? Was God pulling a fast one again? Was this a test? Was it all a test? And if it was, was I going to be rewarded or punished?

The loss hurt, but not as bad as I thought it would. Double overtime and we played our guts out. Our entire team was punch-drunk with effort and exhaustion. Sarah insisted that we lost because her mother washed her lucky underwear. Kit made a gagging gesture. "You mean, you've been wearing the same undies since quarter-finals? Eeew!"

"What?! It's like hockey players not shaving until they win the Stanley Cup!"

I didn't want to think about it.

The championship game was held on neutral territory, so we were at a new venue, Central Secondary. Of course, everybody hunted us down anyway. Even Kit's dad came. He sat with Mama, Papa, the Aunties, and a good smattering of Northern fans. The Aunties, Lord save us, were giving Mr. Cormier basketball pointers. So, ten minutes into it, now duly instructed, Mr. Cormier screamed "FOUL!" whenever an Oakwood player came within two feet of Kit, or more inconveniently, whenever Kit came within two feet of an Oakwood player.

Kit smacked the back of my head in the first quarter. "I am so sorry, buttercup." We walked over to the key for Madison's foul shot. "Sorry for not getting the Mama and Auntie thing at the games." I shrugged. Mr. Cormier waved to her from the bleachers. He expected her to wave back while he was still waving or he'd get frantic. We both waved. "I so get it now, man."

We were hurting as we limped off the court that last time. Our section, our "fans," including all the kids from Northern, stood and clapped us off. They *all* stood up. It was … I mean, a standing O … for losers? Mama and Auntie Luba cried as they waved, cheered, and eventually exited. David gathered us in, his voice hoarse from shouting. He reminded us that Oakwood was older, taller, heavier, and dirtier than we were, and that despite that, we still gave them game. The boy was levitating. I've never seen him smile so much. David congratulated everyone individually, shaking their hands, patting them on the back, clasping their arms. I waited for my turn, heart thumping, from the game I mean.

Would he touch me? How could he not? Of course he would. What would I do? How would that feel?

"Sophie." I braced myself. "Brilliant game, great ball." He raised his hand toward me and then withdrew it like I had the plague. "Awesome effort."

"He's blushing," Madison whispered behind me.

He was. David looked at my knees. His jaw clenched, unclenched, clenched … "Yeah," he said apropos of nothing and marched off.

Madison and I both looked at each other stunned. "Well, at least that's the last I'll see of him," I said. Madison's eyes narrowed.

"I mean it, good riddance. A girl could get whiplash trying to figure him out."

"Or something." She smiled.

We hobbled over to Mike's to lick our wounds with milkshakes and fries. He hugged each of us as we came in. Mike is not a huggy kind of guy. "Luba called. You brats are champions in my eyes."

We slid into our booth with more care than usual. Over milkshakes we decided that it *was* okay. We did the best we could do, played above our heads and above our weight as long as we could. "To next year!" I raised my glass.

"To next year!" We clinked.

"Speaking of next year, Sophie." Mike plopped down the platter of fries. "I'm gonna need ideas for decorating this place for the big do, ya know?"

"Huh?" said Kit. Madison and Sarah lasered me.

"I couldn't stop them," I said.

"Who? What?" asked Sarah.

"THEM," I said.

"The Aunties?" she asked. "What now?"

"It's too stupid for words …"

"Find the words, Sophie," said Madison.

"Aargh!" I groaned. "I went to their last glamour day. Big mistake. Turns out they think it's a tragic miscarriage of justice that I was deprived of my Sweet Sixteen. So, apparently, I'm having it this February."

"You're having your Sweet Sixteen on your seventeenth birthday?" asked Sarah. No one had a firmer grasp of the obvious than Sarah.

"Yeah, but of course it will be billed as my …"

"Sweet Seventeen!" they said in unison.

"Genius!" said Kit. "And it's going to be here? Holy cowpie! That's never been done before. Think of it, ladies, a Sweet Seventeen party at Northern's most preferred eating and drinking establishment and all to ourselves! All sorts of families have tried to buy out Mike over the years for a party. The very best families, Sophie."

"The very *blondest* families, Sophie." Sarah winked.

"Which means that your party will be *beyond* blonde, Sophie Kandinsky." Madison whipped out a pen and started writing on her napkin. "We're going to start a whole new trend with this seventeen thing, I can just feel it."

We? I was being hijacked, again. They were as bad as the Aunties.

"We'll make this the toughest invite to score in years!" Sarah clapped.

"At some point we'll have to arrange for a meeting with the Aunties," said Madison. "A party summit, so to speak."

Why didn't I see it earlier, just because they didn't have accents …

"What's the matter?" Madison put her hand on top of mine.

Mike was loudly scraping the grill, but I knew he was listening. I flashed to the nightmare grade six sleepover, to all those times at recess when I was shoved into the middle of a ring and taunted as the "murderer's kid." School after school, even the teachers looked the other way. I shook my head. I had to fly under the radar, not into it. It was a survival thing. "You don't get it." I paused and looked at each of them. "Whenever I'm at the centre of anything, I end up starring in a horror movie. I've told you guys about some of it. It *never* ends well. A whole party? For me? Humiliation city. It'll suck, how could it not suck?"

Silence.

Madison lit a cigarette. "Sophie, dear," she patted my hand and blew smoke in my face, "don't be a dork. It's tedious. That was then and this is now."

"You're one of *us,* buttercup," said Kit, like that explained everything.

"Don't worry, Soph." Sarah threw her arm around me. "We'll make sure you get the best Sweet Seventeen party in the history of parties! We'll have to black out the windows of course, and remove the loose tables and chairs in the back for dancing, reposition the jukebox, and …"

And they were off. They were *worse* than the Aunties.

By nine o'clock we were too stupid with tiredness to come up with anything useable. Madison looked at her watch. "Sophie's staying over tonight. Sarah, I know you're meeting George, but how about you, Kit? Want to join us?"

Kit looked twitchy. "Can't," she said in some pathetic hope that she could leave it at that.

We all waited. If it took another round of coffee so be it.

"Rick?" asked Sarah helpfully.

"No." Kit shook her head.

We waited some more. Just as Madison was going for the

coffee pot, Kit groaned. "I'm scheduled to have a marathon conversation with my mom."

"That's sweet," said Sarah sweetly.

Madison raised her eyebrow.

Kit sighed and then looked to me. "See, the thing of it is …"

Oh my God, oh my God! Was she going to tell? What should I do? How should I look? How to react? I rearranged my eyebrows into neutral.

"The thing is," she began again, "my mother wants me to move to California this summer and finish high school there."

Silence. Mike went back to scraping the grill. I raised an empty coffee cup to my lips and slurped air.

"Yeah, so?" Madison frowned.

"Yeah?" agreed Sarah. "She gave up that right three years ago!"

"Not even worth thinking about," insisted Madison. "Your life is here with us and with your dad who's knocked himself out trying to be a good mom!"

This had to be why I felt so comfortable with them right off the bat in grade nine. My Blondes had a complete disregard for anything resembling personal boundaries. Your life was their life. I nodded at whoever said anything, terrified that I'd blow it for Kit with the wrong tone or word or look.

"Sophie?" said Madison.

"Stay," I said. Kit blushed and looked at her empty coffee cup. "Tell her you want to stay. I know you miss your mom. I know she can, uh, offer you a different kind of life." Madison and Sarah were nodding even though they couldn't possibly understand what I was trying to say. I wasn't too sure myself. "We'll make up for her, Kit." Vigorous nodding all around, even from Mike behind the counter. "Stay with us until you graduate. There's plenty of time for California and … well, all of that."

"Sure." She shrugged. "I just have to hear her out is all. She's my mom."

"Barely," said Madison, who knew whereof she spoke on that issue.

Kit shot her a look, but Madison did not, would not, back down.

"I'll pray on it for you," I offered.

Unanimous groaning.

"You guys are going to be sorry. When I get to the Pearly Gates, given that I'm so tight with Buddha and the boys, I'll be waved right in."

"Yeah but you'll be lonely without us." Madison elbowed me. "Let's go!"

We slowly limped our sorry, losing butts over to the Chandler manse. It really would have been so much better had that girl passed her driver's test. We went straight for the kitchen as soon as we got in and made more coffee. I pulled up a stool and marvelled at the room all over again. When I first sat here almost three years ago, I thought it was the most beautiful, perfect thing I had ever seen in the world, except for maybe Madison. Creamy cupboards, creamier marble, two white sinks, hand-painted tiles. Nothing bad could ever happen to anyone who had a kitchen like this.

"What are you smiling at?"

She startled me. "You," I said. "Us."

"Yeah." She plopped a bowl of Cheetos in front of me. "Well, on that point, like are you pissed at me or something?"

"Me?"

"Yeah, you! You've been doing distant for weeks. What's up? What did I do?"

"You?"

"Let's not go through this again, yeah me. Are you bummed that I still haven't come clean about Edna? You think I'm such a fake, don't you?"

"Wow." I shoved a fistful of Cheetos in my mouth. "Unbelievable. Madison, you who sat with me for hours pouring me coffee and keeping all those tampons coming until I finally got one in. You who made your grandfather reopen Papa's court case. *And* you who kept the whole Papa in Prison thing a secret until I could figure out how to say the words. Who does that?! What kind of warm turd would I have to be to get all righteous with you? I am actually insulted!"

"Well …" She was trying not to smile. "I guess that *was* pretty fabulous of me. But …"

"Madison, I'll adore you until I die. I don't care how many of your secrets I take to the grave with me." I reached for a Twinkie. "It would be good for you to come clean. But you *know* that. We've talked about it until we were hoarse."

"Double-swear?"

"Hands on heart, swear."

"Then it's you, Sophie. What's up? What *is* going on?"

"I saw him."

"Luke." It wasn't a question. "Other than the church?"

I nodded.

"Other than today?"

"Today?!"

"Yeah, at the game." Madison grabbed a stool and turned around to face me. "He was there for a bit in the first quarter. I thought for sure you knew. Even David saw him and then he left before the quarter ended."

"David saw him?" My throat constricted. "Today? But I didn't feel him, I always feel ..." I sounded goofy even to me. "No, not today, at the park."

"Sophie ..."

"Totally by accident." She folded her arms. "Pretty much. Just a couple of times, nothing happened, Madison. Nothing!"

"What you mean, you *feel* him?"

"It's an electric thing. I can always sense him when he's near."

"Sophie, that is straight out of your cheesy romance novels."

"I don't read them anymore, remember. I got religion instead."

"Well, he didn't even sit. He was in the back row, at the very top. And never mind that. Are you sneaking around with—"

"No!" And without any warning, my eyes burned. "Not really."

Madison reached over and put her hands on my knees. "Sophie ..."

"He is so, so unhappy, Madison. Poor, poor Luke. It's like his life is over."

"Luke made that life, Sophie."

"He loves *me*. Just me, he said so or he said 'there was just me' and I, well, there is just Luke, there will only ever be just Luke, Madison."

I could tell she was trying not to roll her eyes. "He's *married,* Sophie, with a wife and baby. Married."

"I can't help it, Madison. I've tried. I love him." I put my head on the cool, soothing counter. "I'm sure of it. Almost a hundred percent, practically."

"I know when I'm licked." Her shoulders slumped. "Okay, let me know if you need my help."

I threw my arms around her.

"I'm also licked about Edna. You're right. She's wearing me down. I'm going to tell them. Soonish." She nodded to herself. "Enough about that. Let's talk about your party. It's going to be the party of the year, the best night of your life!"

The party again. *My stomach clenched.* I didn't want to talk about the party, think about the party, or plan for the party. It got in the way of my denial about the party. *And unclenched.* She turned to me. "I know you hate the word, Sophie, but I keep my word when I give it." *And clenched.* She grabbed my arm. "Your Sweet Seventeen will be brilliant. You will be brilliant, Sophie Kandinsky. I *promise,*" she said.

17

The first week of December is always brutal at school and beyond brutal at home. It was mid-terms at Northern, a hellish week when all your projects and papers were due, plus the added thrill of exams. That was tolerable. What was *in*tolerable was Mama breathing down my neck every single second I was home. She got anxious during my mid-terms at the best of times, but some fool had gone and told her that marks counted as of now, that universities start looking at what you did in grade eleven. I will hunt that person down and give them cavities.

I looked up from my calculus. She was pacing the living room. Mama rearranged her house-showing schedule just so that she could babysit my studying. I now knew exactly how Papa felt when he was trying to find a job last year. She made me coffees, brought me sandwiches, paced, and asked if she could quiz me, time me, help me, over and over again.

By Friday, when exams were done, I actually contemplated having a drink at Madison's End of Mid-Terms bash. It wasn't supposed to be a party-party per se, it would be looser than that, a last-minute blow-off-some-steam type of deal. She invited less than thirty people, so, less than fifty ought to show. The party was going to be in her pool house way in the back of their yard, which had a slight whiff of danger, especially since she'd somehow got her parents to vacate the premises. Fabi, who would take a bullet for Madison, was supposed to be the adult in charge.

Fabi cleaned up the pool house and rigged it with space heaters while we stocked the mini-fridge and brought in armloads of ice and junk food. Madison insisted that we string up the summer lanterns and she was right. In the snow all softly lit up, it was like we were starring in *Doctor Zhivago*.

Madison just invited Northern kids, well except for George and Mike Jr., who were now a fixture because of Sarah and … was Mike Jr. circling Madison lately? Could be. He was an older boy, so he'd know not to move too fast or he'd scare her off. I felt heat rise off of Madison when he came in and kissed her fingers. Smooth. Of course our entire team was there, plus the "fans" who were loyal enough to come to our championship game. Some of the senior boys basketball team was invited, plus a couple of hockey players, and a stray football player or two. By ten-thirty or so, we had just under sixty kids.

Barbara Sweeton, left guard, second string, was in charge of the music. She and Barbara Barton kept it cool, alternating disco, rock, and seriously slow dance tunes. Kit wandered around passing out mini Christmas cupcakes with a dependably lovesick Rick trailing behind her.

Madison was on the floor dancing with Mike Jr. Sarah was on the floor too, with George, but they were barely moving. I, of course, was with nobody and torqued pretty tight to boot. Something about the architecture of the pool house made you feel the songs more—they vibrated on the floor in a way that travelled up your body and, well, someone should bottle that. When I couldn't stand it a minute longer, I went to the bar. Paul Wexler, who happened to be Madison's next-door neighbour, was nominally in charge.

"Hey, Sophie." He winked at me. "Sorry I couldn't make the game. You look real nice tonight. Different from everybody else, but extra nice, always extra nice."

"Thanks, Paul." I was wearing black jeans and a black boat-neck top with a big wide slit at the neck and shoulders. It was my Audrey Hepburn look and I was about to tell him, but I then realized he wouldn't know what I was talking about. It was Luke who loved old movies. Luke would have got it. I looked at the beers in the cooler, the vodkas and rums lining the bar. Did I want a drink?

"Madison said that if, by some miracle, you ended up looking for something, I was supposed to give you this." Paul disappeared on the other side of the bar and then reappeared with an unopened bottle of Courvoisier and a smile. "Apparently, she's had it and hid it for almost two years." I looked out into the room. It oozed romance, right down to the snow decorating each windowpane on the French doors. Kids were talking, laughing, a group was playing Twister of all things in the corner behind one of the sofas. But mainly there were couples. Couples dancing, couples kissing, couples everywhere. I wanted to be a couple. I wanted to crawl right out of myself. "Yeah, sure, why not? Please pour me a brandy, Paul."

He was only too happy to oblige. Never mind a shot, Paul filled an entire juice glass. That would be more brandy than I'd drunk in my entire life. I'd never even been tipsy before. If I drank that I'd have to be hospitalized.

"Cheers, tiger!" He took a swig of his beer. "I'll demand a dance as my payment."

"Sure." I smiled. Paul was sweet in that tall, blonde, sunburned skier kind of way. Apparently, he raced as well as played football. Maybe I could get myself to like Paul. He winked again.

Then again, maybe not. I looked out into the room. Before I could take a sip, or continue considering how unfulfilled I was feeling, Sarah popped up beside me, beaming blissfully.

"Two more beers, please." She fanned herself. She wasn't wearing a bra. Not good. "Hot in here, ain't it, Soph?"

Warning bells rang around me. We had a real scare with Sarah last year just about at this time. It's like she loses her brains every winter. I leaned over and whispered, "I think we should go to the girls' room."

"I don't have to pee, but if you want some company sure, Soph!"

The lights in the pool house suddenly got dimmer. Someone was playing with them. Our DJs, the Barbaras, were spinning sexy hurtin' tunes. I heard a little yelp, giggling. And then the air changed. David walked in. Well, strode in. Well, as much as anyone can stride anywhere with Janice Wilton clinging to him like Saran Wrap. It was a testament to his strength that David Walter could move at all. The room sparked; everyone noted his arrival. Janice started sucking his face as soon as he plopped down on the sofa. It could turn your stomach.

"Wow," said Sarah. "She won't even let that poor boy catch a breath."

"Yeah, poor boy."

Two other girls joined him and Janice on the overcrowded sofa. David semi-reclined and his retinue rearranged themselves around him. Sandy Thomas minced up to the bar, got four beers, and minced back.

"You know." Sarah couldn't take her eyes off them. I stared at the opposite wall like I was personally responsible for holding it up. "You know," she repeated, "I think our coach is a wee bit loaded. Hmm, looks good on him. But then again, you gotta admit that everything looks good on him. If it weren't for George …"

"Speaking of George, girls' room, Sarah? Not here, the one in the house."

I grabbed my drink and her. The sharp frigid air was a slap in the face compared with the steamy pool house.

"What's going on, Sarah? I know all the signs now. You promised me that you weren't ever going to put yourself in that position again. So to speak."

She didn't say anything until we got to the house. "I know I said I wouldn't, Sophie."

My stomach seized. I was still spooked from last year's five-alarm pregnancy scare, but not so our Sarah. "Holy

Moses, Sarah, you promised!" There was that word again. "I can't take it! Have you and George, don't tell me you …"

"No!" She yanked me into the main floor powder room and shut the door. "Not yet, I mean. I, we haven't and I wouldn't tonight, honestly, but see the thing of it is …"

"What do you mean *but*? Sarah, we can't go through that again!"

She jumped up and sat on the vanity counter. "Oh hose yourself down. You're wound up tighter than a copper coil. What you need is a good, uh, romance."

"Sarah Davis, you're drunk!"

"Oh Lord, just a little, and when did you turn into such a priss?" She faced the mirror and played with her hair.

"Sarah?"

"Relax." She swung back to me. "I haven't, but one day, maybe soon, we may, and I want to be prepared this time. I read all about it in those pamphlets you got me from Planned Parenthood last year. Condoms, I mean. I'm actually going to buy them and make him wear them, I swear. I'm never, ever going to go through a nightmare like last year again. Like how mature and super responsible is that?"

I took a big swig of brandy.

"And you're going to help."

And then another swig.

"We have to go somewhere where no one could possibly recognize us and buy some. Plan? I'll be seventeen in March, that's practically an adult, after all. How about tomorrow?"

I pulled down the toilet seat lid and sat. Holy crap.

"I really, really like him, Soph. How about after you're finished at Mike's?"

"I guess," I groaned. "I mean, if you're bound and determined, I suppose it's better than—"

"That's my Soph." She jumped off the counter. "Tomorrow, four-thirty, at Bathurst station!" And then she dashed off, leaving me in the can, so to speak. Priss? Did she say I was prissy? I took another sip and then got up. "Prissy?" I snorted. Then I realized I'd said it out loud. "It's just me, Fabi!" I said to the hallway. "I'm going back to the party now."

I took another sip and noted that I was feeling nice and warmish in the various bits of me. As if anyone cared.

Not true, Paul had looked like he cared. Maybe I *could* make myself care that he cared. I stepped back outside into the yard. Took another sip as I picked my way through the snow and tried to imagine Paul holding me. I shuddered.

I was almost at the pool house, just about to reach for the door handle, when *he* grabbed me and spun me around with such force that I dropped my drink in the snow.

"Sophie!" His voice blistered the stone-cold air. "Sophie." Somehow one hand was holding my head and the other was behind my back. David crushed me into him and against the outside wall. I opened my mouth to yell at him, but he covered it with his lips. "Sophie," softer now, "Sophie." I felt delirious in that kiss. I was stunned. Everything turned. It was like being on a free-floating carousel. I have never been held like that, felt like that. I should be furious, yet … damn. I was in love with Luke! It was *not* possible that I was feeling what I was feeling. David's hands were at first like a vise, then stroking, then caressing, then almost not touching me. Is *this* what *this* feels like? My body was so disloyal. How could I do this to me!? He traced my face and neck with the tips of his fingers, caressing one small part of me at a time, making the rest scream out in protest. I should resist, make more of a show, at least pretend. Then his lips were on me again.

I knew from watching him all these months that no one was stronger. He bit my lip tenderly, teasing me before forcing my mouth open again. David's hand glided down to the small of my back. He pulled me into his body with a force that stole my breath and my brains because somewhere, somehow I was kissing him back. If that's what we were doing. He made my body mould to his, fit into him. He was too practised, much too aware of exactly what he was doing and its effect. There wasn't a square inch of me that wasn't lit up. The snow sizzled around us.

David yanked my sleeve, pulling the top away from my neck and shoulder. He let go of my mouth and I reached out, wanting to grab him to me again, the shock of him detaching was so great. He looked at me and groaned. Then he licked and nipped the crook of my neck, travelling up and down from my ear to the top of my chest, my shoulder while his hands were on me. *I almost passed out.* David's mouth crushed mine again, rough and angry. And then, just as I lost myself in him, he growled, his voice so low and gravelled, I could barely make out his words.

"So tell me, Sophie," he whispered. "Are you tired of being Luke's little something on the side?"

He might as well have thrown me in the snow. Without

missing a beat, I hauled off and slapped David Walter with everything I had.

It took both of us by surprise.

He let go of me, of course. A canyon opened up between us. The humiliation, the shame of it was that I wanted to pull back into him more than I wanted to breathe.

"Whoa." David brought his hand to his face and almost smiled. "Good arm."

I looked through the French doors into the party. Janice was combing the room for him.

"I'm ... I've had too much to drink." He sucked in some air, whistled. "Just too ... No. I apologize, Sophie. Damn!" He looked up at the night sky. "I'm an ass and there is no excuse. God, I'm sorry."

Fine. I lose my head to a guy who's so plastered he doesn't know what he's doing. What was the matter with me? My body betrayed me! Totally. Enough already. I couldn't count on anyone, especially me. Dear God, I wanted to hug him and hit him, hug him and hit him, hug him and forget it. I was reeling.

David reached for me and stopped. "I mean that. I sincerely and completely apologize." He ran his hands through his hair. "I have never ..."

"Ivory soap," I said. I thought that maybe if I said stuff, I would stop swirling, stop feeling those feelings.

He exhaled. Didn't say anything for a while. "Pardon?"

"You use Ivory soap."

David stepped closer then stepped back again. "Damn," he muttered. "How do you know? My mom says it isn't supposed to smell like anything."

His mom? Somehow that was startling. "It doesn't," I said. "You just smell like you." I was trying to cycle myself down, get control over any part of me. The scent of him wasn't helping. I stepped back.

"God, Sophie, I'm so—"

I put up my hand. "S'okay, David, I'm not going to report you or anything." I looked back into the party. My head spun, full as it was of brandy, or of David. "Your, um, friends, are looking for you."

David stepped toward me and then he stepped back. He was remembering those girls in there, what they could and would do for him. He nodded, stepped back even farther. Angry? Then he turned and went back into the party. Yup, angry.

What the hell?

I left. As soon as I could walk properly that is. Holy Moses, enough was enough. I was tired. It was almost midnight. I didn't say goodbye. I didn't even go in after my purse.

Mama was home. The door would be unlocked. I walked the whole way in some lame attempt to cool off, calm down, and stop feeling so wired. It didn't work. I was practically levitating.

As soon as I got in, at almost one, Mama popped up from the couch, ready to pretend she was watching the test pattern for the Buffalo channel. She had done this every single night since Papa left. "Did you have lots of fun and celebrations at da party?"

"You bet, Mama." I bit my lip. *Ow.* It was swollen. "But I'm exhausted. Good night."

Back in my room I sat my sorry butt on the bed, didn't move. Well, except for turning my brand-new little Buddha statue around, so he wasn't looking at me. I didn't get changed, nothing. I traced the shape of my lips with my index finger over and over again. You don't get more pathetic than me. I was angry and ashamed of myself on so many different levels, I couldn't even begin to sort it out. Even worse, way worse, I couldn't stop thinking about it, about him, and of course that made me mental. But still, *even worser* than any of that, was when I looked back and saw Janice Wilton jumping into his arms before he could even shut the door, followed by the picture of David Walter kissing her back like he was starving.

I checked my makeup in between serving customers at Mike's. My lips were swollen when I got up and they were still in full bloom at the restaurant. And that wasn't the worst of it. David had marked me! How could he? How dare he! I had a hickey! Well, two actually, both in the crook of my neck. They stared at me accusingly when I got up and they kept staring back and shaming me every time I pulled down my turtleneck in Mike's restroom.

"You okay, kid?" Mike asked when I returned from my 157th hickey check.

"Sure." I nodded. "End-of-term party at Madison's last night, you know?"

Mike grunted, reached over, and pounded the cash register. When it slid open, he reached for two packets, threw the tablets into a glass and filled it with water. "It's our secret, kid."

Alka-Seltzer was not going to help my hickeys any, but I

could hardly explain that to Mike. "Thanks." I gulped down the bubbling fizz in one shot.

I was still burping on my way to the park. What was in that stuff? I checked my watch and sat on the bench, our bench. Would he come? Would he know to come? How long should I wait? What the hell was I doing? Twenty minutes passed. This was nuts. I was nuts. Well, that much was irrefutably proven last night; this was just the icing on the proof, or something.

I felt him before I could see him. It was always like that, but only when it came to Luke.

My hickeys throbbed. Okay, and David too, but only in a bad way.

Luke came up behind me and kissed the top of my head, right there, in public and in front of everyone, including his old guys three benches over. He reached around in front of me flourishing a Styrofoam coffee cup. "Double-double for my angel."

"Goody," I said.

"How are you?" He leapt right over the back of the bench. My heart snagged on something sharp, that careless goofy grace, showing off and not even realizing it. Doing it just because you could was so something high school boys did. Not a married man and a father.

"I'm good." I just wanted to sit and soak him in while he smiled at me. "What's up? You look excited."

"I am I guess." He shrugged. "I've just completed all my qualifying courses to start a part-time diploma at Ryerson in January."

"Great!" I hugged him. A whoosh of guilt swamped me. Was that adultery? Okay, maybe not, but there was a whole other commandment about coveting and that hug definitely felt like a coveting-type thing. I let go.

"Yeah, so the marketing program is where it's at, you know?"

I nodded. "Like advertising?"

He pulled off the lid to his coffee and raised it to the old guys. They raised theirs. Quite the little ritual. "Yeah, that's what my old man does."

"Advertising?"

"It's his firm, so one day it'll be mine, right? I'll just get this dink certificate and onward and upward, you know?"

My neck pulsed. I could feel heat rising off my hickeys. Should I ask? No. None of my business, absolutely, none of my … "What happened between you and David Walter?" I was as surprised as he was that it came out. I was even more surprised to see him look away. He examined his running shoes for quite some time. "Why? Did he say anything?"

"No." I shook my head. "It's just that you two were so tight and now, well, like did he just desert you?"

Luke's little something on the side.

My hand flew to my throat.

Luke shook his head. "Naw, it wasn't like that." He finished his coffee. "See, David always wanted what I had." He looked at me. "*And* he wanted Alison, you know?"

Something unplugged in me. David and Alison Hoover? Alison double-D black-eyeliner Hoover? "But …"

"Yeah, I know you're thinking that David has pretty much

had any girl he wanted. But thing is, he wanted Alison because she was *mine*. It was always like that between us, ever since we were kids."

But, Alison Hoover? Okay, I thought. Maybe, yeah, sure, that might make sense....

"David was always jealous of me. He didn't know I was going to end it with her." Luke reached over, stroked my cheek.

I dissolved into his fingers.

"End it and be with you." He leaned closer. "If he knew about you, Sophie, he'd come after you just to be another notch on his belt." Luke touched my hair, brushing it behind my shoulder, lingering. "And to get back at me. He doesn't know about us, does he?"

Luke's little something on the side. I felt sick. It explained everything. Shame pitched around in me like I was a pinball machine. I shook my head.

"Good, keep it that way. Keep far away from him, Sophie. Your coach is no angel."

Okay, right, that was for sure, but even in my re-adoration of Lucas Pearson, it hit me that he wasn't exactly a candidate for the priesthood either.

"... and it won't be forever. My dad's on the case, and like I said, I'll be at the firm in no time and cut loose. I'll have done my time. But, meanwhile, there's us. I can't stand being away from you, Sophie." He put his arm on the back of the bench and leaned in even closer. "I so want, need, to touch you again, to know if you'll wait for me. Meet me somewhere, anywhere, more private. Meet me, Sophie, so I know I have you to keep me going. I need you. At least promise that we can meet here again to talk about it some more." I inhaled the scent of coffee and cream on his lips. "Please, Sophie."

He *needed* me. Lucas Pearson needed me, needed *me*.

"Just nod, and we can work it out later, Sophie. Say we'll meet here again and that will let me get through Christmas. I won't make it without you. That will be my present. No shopping, no gift boxes, just you."

Shopping! I jumped. "Got to go! I'm meeting Sarah at the Bathurst subway station. We're going to … buy stuff."

He grabbed my wrist. "Say it, Sophie. Say we'll meet again."

I got up.

"Say we'll meet!"

I slipped my hand out before turning toward the subway station. I looked back at him looking at me. "We'll meet!"

"When?" he called.

"January, the middle of the month!"

"I'll be here every Saturday in January, just in case. Merry Christmas! I'll be waiting!"

I broke into a run with my heart erupting. I tried to grab hold of myself while I ran down the steps to the subway. That whole episode scared me. Hell, I scared me. What did I just agree to exactly? What in Buddha's name was I doing? And just as bewildering, David, jealous of Luke? David wanted Alison? It didn't make sense, but then, who cares? Not me. I had enough on my messy moral plate. So I went back to obsessing about what it was I had agreed to with Luke and how much trouble I was going to get into because I had agreed to whatever it was.

When I finally stumbled out and into the station, all that

stuff left. The Bathurst subway station! I was almost run over by the rush of memories.

"Over here!" Sarah waved by the doors. "What are you smiling at?"

"I think I used to live around here."

"You *think*?"

"A long time ago," I said. "We moved a million times right after Papa was sentenced. It gets confusing."

Sarah slipped her arm through mine. "Sorry. So when was this?"

"This." I turned and led Sarah on to one of the residential streets, Euclid Avenue. "*This* was before that. Euclid was before prison, before drinking, well, that's not completely true, but before prison for sure. Euclid was when we were happy." She squeezed my arm into her. "Do you mind walking a bit? I want to find my home. We're close, I think."

Sara nodded while rifling through her big bag. She pulled out my purse. "You left this at Madison's. Where did you take off to?"

"Thanks," I said. "I'm surprised you noticed, what with you and George sucking in the same oxygen and all."

She let that pass. "How could I not notice when our assistant coach kept rousting around and demanding to know where you were."

"David?" The hickeys throbbed on cue. How annoying was that?

"Yeah." She nodded. "Something happen between the two of you? I mean something other than you throwing rocks at each other?"

Being pulled into him. "We had words," I said.

"You are the most combustible couple in the whole school."

"What the hell, Sarah! We are *not* a couple."

She stopped in her tracks, and since she had me by the arm, she stopped me too. "Whoa, where there's that much smoke …" She put up her hand. "It seemed like he was worried is all. He kept asking if you often went home alone, how far away was it, did you usually walk, et cetera, et cetera. I'm telling you, Janice was steamed. She was ready to do him right then and there."

"So, did he leave with her?"

"Why on earth would you care, Sophie?" She dug her elbow into my side.

"I don't. Not a bit. I'm not another notch."

"Huh?"

"Nothing. Did you know that he's always been jealous of Luke?" Sarah looked skeptical. "Everybody says so."

She shook her head. "That just doesn't seem right. Half the girls in the known universe are panting after him. Madison could find out …"

"No!" We started walking again. "I mean, who cares either way, right? Let's just walk, okay? It's so good to be home." I looked up. "Euclid Avenue. This is it, Sarah. My street."

"Cool! Which one was your home?"

Yes, which one? "Number 362?" We walked up to 362. Tidy and tightly bunched semi-detached homes lined both sides of the street, each a replica of the other. In the summer, instead of front lawns, little rectangles teemed with dahlias and preening gladiolas mixed in among beefsteak tomatoes and monster zucchinis. Every slit of a veranda had at least three chairs for sitting on, for observing and inserting yourself into street theatre.

Was this it? Could be, but … it was always summer in my memories and now the gardens were buried in greying snow. The fences had changed, paint colours were updated. It threw everything off.

"Is this your house, Sophie?"

"I don't know! My God, I really *don't* know. How is that possible? It was in my head all these years. Home, the last place I was happy …" I walked over to number 364, back to 362, then to 366 and back to 364.

"Sophie?"

"I don't know, Sarah. I just don't know." My heart raced. "It's all so different, but not! I can't tell which one's my house." Tears bullied their way up to my eyes. "It was so important, this house where we *all* lived. This was home and now I can't even find it! I've lost my home."

"No you haven't, you dope!" Sarah threw her arms around me. "What are you talking about? You have a home with Mama and us and the Aunties and even Papa."

I groaned.

"It's true! This," she flicked her hand at the houses, "whichever one it's supposed to be, is not your home. *We're* your home." She grabbed a wadded-up Kleenex out of her pocket and gave it to me. "Get it?"

It took forever just to unfurl the Kleenex. "Yeah." I blew into it. "Sorry, I've been a wreck lately." I blew again. She looked skeptical. "No really, let's go. Time for Honest Ed's!"

We marched back to Bloor Street, but not so fast that I wasn't whiplashed by how different the people looked. This neighbourhood was one of those long-established and long-suffering entry points for Canada's immigrants. So, of course, just about everyone looked like they came from some unpronounceable place, but that wasn't it. On Bloor and Bay, it was the seventies: maxi dresses, wide-leg pants, perms, psychedelic colours. On Bloor and Bathurst, it was still the fifties: narrow ties, housedresses, fake pearls, and real gold.

And in Honest Ed's, it was the land that time forgot.

"Wow!" said Sarah when we stepped in. She couldn't navigate the rabbit's warren of aisles, half floors, and stairs that didn't seem to go anywhere. I grabbed Sarah and yanked her through aisles of tables loaded down with copper pots, men's underwear, and packages of Epsom salts. I pulled her down one set of stairs and up the other, until we got to the pharmacy, and then I inhaled and walked straight over to the pharmacist, like my old librarian friend, Mrs. Theodora Setterington, had coached me to last year.

"Excuse me, sir. We'd like to buy some condoms, please."

Sarah squealed and would have run off, but I had a death grip on her ski jacket. The pharmacist, an ancient-mariner-type guy, just looked at us, from Sarah to me and back to Sarah. Okay, this could go so wrong.

"Sheepskin or latex?"

We looked at each other. "Eeew, they kill Lamb Chop for this?" Sarah whimpered.

"Latex, please," I said.

"Do you think that a box of eighteen will be, uh, adequate?"

Sarah wanted to bolt again. I held tight.

"Yes, sir. Thank you, sir."

I reached for the box but he took it back. "I think you may want to pay for it here." He nodded his head at Sarah. "She's not gonna make it through the front checkout line."

He had a point. Sarah was whiter than a toilet bowl. "Yes, sir. Thank you so much, sir." I gave him a twenty and he fixed us up.

We bolted out of Honest Ed's like our butts were on fire. Back on Bloor Street we allowed ourselves a little victory dance.

And then the skies opened up and it started to pour. Sarah and I tore off laughing for no good reason, all the way to the subway station. The rain came down in sheets punctured by the occasional lightning bolt. It was December and this kind of storm was strange. I couldn't help feeling that it was some kind of major sign, except I couldn't figure out the message. I was a mess of guilt and good—good guilt? Given what I had just done for Sarah, what had happened with Luke earlier, and what had happened with David last night, God and everybody living on my altar were either spitting on me or absolving me of my sins. Thing is, if a verdict came in at that moment, I had a nagging feeling that I'd come out way more sinner than saint.

I dreamed about him last night, again. David I mean. It was humiliating. Every night I'd go to bed thinking about Luke, Christmas presents, and Papa, and then I'd toss and turn under David's hands on me.

Even in my dreams he's all superior and despicable. I needed an exorcism. If I could just put him in his place. After I brushed my teeth, I went to Papa's mirror where I do all my best posing. I visualize myself walking into the library and bumping into David. I toss my hair just so, as he says, "Hey, Sophie, what a surprise meeting you here." He drinks me in all lazy-like, which of course offends me, so I retort with flashing eyes and nostrils flaring. No, that was probably too Harlequin romance, too *Sweet Savage Love*. I check the mirror. It definitely looks like I'm having a spasm; have to work on that. Anyway, with flashing eyes and *barely* flaring nostrils, I *retort* charmingly, "Yes, David, shocking isn't it? I can read!"

Hmmm, a titch too hostile. I make him look hurt though, which I like, a lot. I spend the next twenty minutes trying out different poses in reaction to what David might say. I smile, I sparkle, I gasp with thoughtful concern, all this while sharing bracingly intelligent repartee about America's exit strategy from Vietnam. I'd have to go to the library and get stuff about America's exit strategy or some other big-brain item that I'd floor him with. The girl in the mirror looked skeptical.

I could hardly blame her. I turned and went to my altar, turned my Buddha back around, lit the candle, and started praying, hard.

Dear Everybody, please forgive me for all my impure thoughts, my inclination for revenge, and for thinking about myself so much. I ask you for blessings for my family and friends and, if one of you is not too busy with the world's more pressing problems, could you please make sure that Papa never takes a drink again and comes home very, very soon.

Thank you, thank you.

Amen.

I thought about tacking on the AA prayer about changing the things you can change and leaving the rest alone, but the phone rang. I blew out the candle and ran to get it.

"Buboola, baby, sveetie!"

"Hi Auntie Eva."

"Your Mama is to home?"

"Nope, either at the office or showing houses."

"Tell her zat for sure I'm vanting to do za Christmas dinner here, vit everybodies." Long pause. "It vill help vit za engraving."

"You mean, grieving?"

"*Zat* is vat I said."

"Sorry, I misheard."

"Iz okay. You are okay, buboola?"

I shrugged and then realized that she couldn't see me shrugging. "Yeah."

"You don't sound happy enough."

"Happy *enough*?"

"*Da!* Christmas is coming, your parents are behaving nice, you are beautiful, *and* you are young."

"Yeah, that's a lot." I had to agree.

"You must be young for all of us, baby buboola."

"Whoa, too much pressure, Auntie Eva! Why don't you guys just relive your own youth?"

Nothing.

"Auntie Eva?"

"Sorry, darrrling. You don't know because ve don't told you. Ve ver never young, not really. Zer vas za var, zer vas za Communists, za fascists. Zer vas too many knockings on za doors in za night, for Radmila, Luba, and your Mama."

"And you too."

"And me too."

I did not deserve to breathe. "I'm sorry, Auntie Eva. I knew a bit, even though you guys don't talk about that stuff. I am so, so sorry!"

"No, no, no, stop! Iz finished, kaput! And ve are having a party!"

"Okay, so, about that."

"Madison and me sent out za invitations, but it must be a secret surprise."

"But it's almost two months away!"

"Ve vant to make it sure."

I would have to kill Madison. She should know better than to get caught up in an Auntie frenzy.

"Already, za peoples are saying zey are coming and zey are exploding vit za excitement."

Okay, maybe too late to pull the party plug. "Uncle," I whimpered.

"*Da,* Uncle Mike vill be zer, *pa* sure, iz his restaurant, and Uncle Dragan too, but ve old people vill be gone, I hope to die, by za midnight."

I started to hyperventilate. A guest list, invites going out, people coming. *Everyone staring at me. And then the big bad thing would happen.* "Who did you ask?" I heard rustling and shuffling.

"I have it here in my hands your list. Za old people you know."

I nodded, my stomach tightened.

"Your basketball team and za boyfriends, ahhh, za nephews, peoples from your English and chemistry class. Some boys from za football, some senior boys, ahhh …" crinkle, shuffle, "some senior basketball boys …" Tighter, tighter, tighter … "Valter David of course!"

"NO! Don't!"

"Yes! Vat no? Vhy not?"

"He won't come!"

"Darrrling buboola, he vas za first von to say he's coming for sure! Absolutely!"

What a mess. Was he going to bring a date? An entourage? I couldn't bring myself to ask. It would be humiliating to ask and that boy had humiliated me enough. Besides, I didn't care. Who cares? Nobody.

"Ve, za Aunties and za Blondes and your Mama for sure, are to have a very top secret, for my eyes only, planning for za decorations, for za music, za food, et cetera, et cetera, et cetera."

I was doomed. All those people, watching and waiting for some Sophie-sized disaster that I was sure I could deliver on. We might as well film it.

"Uncle Dragan is going to bring his movie camera." I suppose they'd notice if I wasn't there. "It vill be for sure za sveetest Sveet Seventeen party!"

I heard her snuffling into a handkerchief. "Yes, Auntie Eva, it will. I can feel it now. I'm sorry I wasn't excited enough earlier. I'm excited, now." Dear Lord. "Now that you've explained it all to me."

Snuffle, snuffle. "You are for sure don't lying."

"I am for sure not lying," I lied.

"And you vill be Sveet Seventeen for all of us?"

I thought about them conniving and conspiring at Auntie Eva's dining room table. My motley crew of Aunties and Blondes.

It was just one night. I've survived worse. "Can't wait," I said.

As soon as I hung up, Mama and Madison burst through the door.

"Look vat I found it in da elevators!" Mama pointed to Madison like she was a lucky penny.

"Mama, call Auntie Eva." I glared at Madison.

Madison followed me into my room almost sheepishly until she actually got there, and then she looked around like she was seeing it for the first time. What was it with everyone and my room this year? You'd think they'd been coming to another Sophie's bedroom all these years. My little altar was like this island of perfect prettiness plopped onto a moonscape. She wrinkled her nose.

"Sophie, isn't it time that you ..."

"Never mind that, Madison. You guys had a party summit with the Aunties?" I crossed my arms. At least she had the good grace to look sheepish again. And then she remembered who she was.

"Have you met your Aunties, Sophie Kandinsky? When was the last time you successfully stood up to them and said no? Name once!"

I didn't say anything.

"Humph, I thought so, and while I've got you in the proper frame of mind about just how persuasive they can be, we, uh, agreed on a fifties theme. Your Sweet Seventeen is going to be a sock hop, just like on *Happy Days*."

"WHAT?"

"It was their idea, but it's good. Everyone loves that show, and we're all going to rent poodle skirts at Malabar. We'll get fitted in January."

I started to vibrate, discreetly.

"And it will be so groovy having everyone in costume, all that fifties music, just think of it!"

I agreed, but I wasn't through sulking and fuming. "How am I supposed to turn up all poodle-skirted and ponytailed when this thing is a surprise?"

"Oh, Sophie, everyone knows that a secret surprise party is never a surprise, or how can the guest of honour possibly look appropriately turned out? I mean *really*."

There was just so much I didn't know. "So, this meeting was last week?"

"Yesterday," she said.

Yesterday? "But Auntie Eva said she already heard from David and that he was coming!"

"Hey, this is cool." Madison picked up my rosary beads and began examining them closely. "Well, she mailed the invites this morning, but Auntie Eva sort of called him special yesterday."

"Oh Jesus H … Madison!"

"I had to give her his number! It was like standing in front of an oncoming train!" she pleaded. "I swear on your altar!"

"Fine, then." I fell onto my bed. "I am going to have to leave the country."

She fell beside me. "He said sure right off."

"Aargh! He'll find a fresh way to humiliate me."

"Oh come on, Sophie. I'm actually coming over to Sarah's point of view on that one, and I think …"

"He knows about Luke."

Silence. We let that sit for a while.

"How?"

"Haven't a clue, but at your party ... never mind. I can't talk about that now. Let's talk about something else, anything else."

She moved over closer. "I know Kit is holding something back."

I got up and started rearranging my altar.

"It's not the puking and it's not California. So ..."

I wanted to tell her so, so much. I wanted to at least prep her, to give my friend some lead time in accepting the big thing about my other friend. If nothing else, it would maybe soften the reaction when and if it came. No not if. Kit would tell her. She would tell them all, and it was Kit's to tell. Still, on the not-so-altruistic front ... it was such a juicy big thing and I was desperate to tell her, watch her shock, have her marvel that I knew. I could feel the words coming up and reaching for air ... and I switched them. "I saw Luke again and he's asked me to meet more, uh, where we'll have, more privacy. And I think I'm going to."

"Oh my God, *Sophie!*"

"Not right away or anything. We're still going to meet at the park next time. He loves me, Madison." I remembered the double-double coffee and winced. "Anyway, he's got this whole plan for his life, his education, me."

Madison sort of smiled but she also sort of looked angry, or disgusted, or sad around the edges. I couldn't tell which one, but it was one of them.

"I gotta go. I just came to give you the heads-up about the fifties thing. Edna's back at the house." There was a lump of quiet between us as we walked to the elevator. When the elevator opened, it startled us both. She got on and then, without warning, she jumped back out and hugged me. "You deserve better, Sophie Kandinsky." Then she stepped back in.

"Easy for you to say," I said to the elevator doors.

It was the prettiest Christmas tree we ever had, large and fat and full, but getting it up and into the elevator was a monster challenge. Once we got it in we had to stop at every floor, given that the branches kept pressing all the buttons, but we did it. Papa stayed around to string it with our seventy-two thousand multi-coloured lights. Every time we moved, Mama and I thought we'd forgotten the Christmas lights and we'd buy a new box. By the time we got to the condo, we had enough to light up City Hall. Where we lost money on new lights, we saved on actual decorations since they were all made by me. I was a glutton with a glue gun, and Mama had packed away every single questionable creation. The total effect was one of being a well-lit mess and, still, it was the prettiest Christmas tree we ever had.

Papa was around a bit more throughout the holidays, not enough, but more. His presence quieted me like a blanket of snow. He seemed to have the opposite effect on Mama. Whenever Papa came by, she flitted around the room like a hummingbird on uppers. For my Christmas present, Papa bought me a copy of the Bhagavad Gita, the Koran, and the Tao Te Ching, translated of course. They were so gorgeous I didn't have the heart to tell him that I wasn't doing any of those. In fact, the books were so pretty that, rather than correct him, I instantly decided I would add a drop of Hindu, Muslim, and Taoism into my spiritual practice. When I had the time.

Papa smiled across our living room, tracked me as I unwrapped each package and fingered the pretty gilt on the tissue-like pages. "They're beyond beautiful, Papa. Thank you so, so much!"

He couldn't contain himself anymore. Papa strode over and crouched down beside me on the floor. "Princessa." He sighed. "Sophie, I *know* you prefer to be called Sophie rather than Sophia. I *know* you like all your coffees black and very sweet, and I *know* you're trying to be somewhat faithful to a blend of Buddhism, reform Judaism, and even some Catholicism." He picked up the Koran. "These, these are for your future." He kissed my forehead. "I think that you will always quest. I also think that those of us who are blessed to be near you will be rewarded by your quests. I'm proud of you, Sophie."

Proud. I gulped down a shot of shame remembering the last few months with Luke and the things I'd contemplated doing with Luke, was still contemplating. It wouldn't stay down. I didn't know where to look. I was playing with doing stuff that wasn't okay in anybody's holy book, no matter how many religions I rifled through or blended together. But, then again, Luke was my everything, the real deal, pure love. Everything was righteous in the name of pure love, right?

Right.

I finally looked up into my father's clear blue eyes. "Yeah well, me too you, Papa."

Mama, not to be outdone, presented me with a little silver menorah on the first night of Hanukkah and followed up on Christmas with my very own *L'Air Du Temps Eau de Parfum,* complete with intertwined crystal swallows. I put a drop on my wrist right away. I smelled like gardenias and fairy tales for the rest of the day.

The Aunties got together and presented me with "cash monies" at Christmas Day dinner at Auntie Eva's. They said that I could spend it any way I liked. Two hundred dollars! They gave me two hundred dollars! I could buy a car or something.

Sarah bought me a stash of Yardley Pot O' Glosses in every shade there was, and Kit gave me a gorgeous mood ring that she swore she got in self-defence to give her a head's-up on how crazy I was in any given moment. Madison floored me. She gave me a 1977 diary just like the one she had, only, instead of being in her buttery turquoise leather with silver engraving, mine was a buttery purple and it was engraved in gold; *Sophie's Secrets* it said. Jesus. I didn't even know that purple was my favourite colour until I saw it there with my name on it.

I didn't deserve any of it.

And then Luke called.

After all this time and all this drama, it was the first time Luke had ever called me. He called on the first week of January, the first day back at school, at 4:14 P.M. I noted it in my purple diary. I guess his coast was clear. He said he'd had my phone number memorized for over a year. My heart throbbed in my throat from the "Hi Sophie" on. I could barely hear him in all that pounding. I listened, recording the sound of his voice in my head while I imagined him, imagined us. It was exhausting.

Even while we were talking it dawned on me that this is how it would have been, *should* have been, if we were just a normal boy and girl. I would giggle too much, even though I wasn't much of a giggler, and move my hands around too much, even though it was just a telephone conversation. His voice would roll over me like spring fog. My boyfriend would call and we would arrange to meet at the park on Saturday, January 15, right after my shift at Mike's. That's what a normal boyfriend and girlfriend would plan on the phone, and that's what we did. I don't remember the rest of the holidays, what I did or with who. I don't remember that first week back at school. I don't even remember doing anything with the Blondes.

I do remember not telling them about any of this.

On January 15, I shot out of Mike's the moment my shift was over. I ran in my boots, parka, and scarves. I should've worn a hat, but I'd look like a dork. Couldn't risk it. When I got to the top of the reservoir, it was clear that we'd have the park to ourselves. All I could hear was my own breathing in that weird way you can when it's freezing and you're all covered up. The snow was blinding, lit by the late afternoon sun, and, even though there was no wind, the air still pierced you. "Too cold to snow," as Auntie Eva used to say. "Too cold to cry."

I practised a head-spinning series of poses. How do you look fetching in so much fake down?

At 3:25, I saw him coming up toward me over the rise and waited, sucking in my stomach the whole time. Luke wore his Northern Varsity jacket. No hat, no scarf, no gloves. He smiled the whole way.

"You're here," he said and reached for me.

"Of course I am." I stepped back. God he was lovely.

I wanted to trace his face with my fingers. Instead he took my arm, and we walked over to the biggest and best oak tree.

"How was Christmas?" he asked.

"Good. Great. I got some amazing gifts, an engraved diary, this bottle of perfume from Mama, brilliant things for my altar." Then I remembered he didn't know anything about my altar. He wouldn't know what I was talking about. Luke smiled, one dimple declaring itself. He didn't ask. He leaned into me, resting an arm against the tree trunk.

It was hard to think. "How about you?" I said it automatically, realizing too late that I so did not want to know. *Don't answer!*

"Okay." He shrugged.

Stop! Stop! No more....

"Mainly with my folks, you know. The baby was fun, I guess." He leaned in closer.

The baby. Their baby. Luke's baby. I felt nauseated and clammy, like you do right before you hurl.

Luke did not take his eyes off me. He was searching for something while telling me how he would be working for his dad by this time next year.

At 3:31, he asked me to come over to his apartment.

"They're gone," he said. "She took the baby to her grandmother's place in Simcoe. Gone for the whole week."

When I was six, after much pleading and visible begging, Mama gave me a nickel for a kiddie ride, the mechanical horse at the Woolworth's five-and-dime store.

"We'll be alone."

The horse threw me, impossible, but true. Somehow I went flying over the front of the stupid thing and I swear, I landed on my stomach at the other end of the store. The sucker-punch of pain from the wind being knocked clean out of me was stunning.

This was like that.

"Just you and me."

Who was he? Who did he think I was? What was I doing here? He had a baby.

"I ..." I shook my head. I just couldn't quite get a grip on the breathing thing.

Luke leaned against me, body on body, well, parka on leather jacket.

"Come home with me."

Home? No matter how hard he cleaned up, they would be there. All these weeks, I had successfully blocked any images about his life with her. But now that I had started, I couldn't get the pictures out of my head. There would be baby paraphernalia everywhere. I saw Alison's hairspray in the bathroom, her cheap dangly earrings on the coffee table. I could smell her stale cologne on the sofa pillows. Mrs. Lucas Pearson might as well be sitting there. How could he ask?

At 3:42 Luke told me he loved me.

If I could just get one normal decent breath. "No you don't," I gasped.

"Sophie, are you okay?"

"No!" I pushed him off me. "You don't even know who I am." He didn't. He couldn't. How could he, when I didn't know myself? But what we were became crystal clear in a heartbeat. The *realness* of what we were doing, of what he was asking, barged in and dirtied the innocent, but doomed, romantic fantasies I'd been playing non-stop in my head since I had caught sight of him at Luigi's funeral. This was not my *L'Air du Temps*. We were not in a field of gardenias and fairy tales.

Luke pulled me to him again. "I know you enough to love you, Sophie."

"Let go." He didn't. "You don't love me, Luke. You love the *idea* of me."

I finally took in a deep breath and exhaled, perfectly. The truth did that. "You never got a chance to love me."

He let go.

"*We* never got a chance." I put my hand against his chest. "And this … what you're asking … I can't. I'm too young to be so old."

"Sophie—"

"I'm going to be seventeen next month," I interrupted. "And there's going to be a party. Bet you didn't know about

either of those things. How could you? I'm going to be
seventeen, Luke, and I want to be seventeen. Seventeen, not
thirty-seven. I've been too old for too long, cleaning up after
my dad, prison, the moves, Mama's moods." I pushed him
away. "I just want to be seventeen, you know?"

He shook his head.

"I *deserve* to be seventeen!"

Luke looked gutted. I wanted to snatch the words back
and throw myself into him, but instead I exhaled again. "You,
because of her …" I waved my arms pathetically. "You have
to be a grown-up now. Luke, you're a *father,* somebody's papa.
You can't escape into me."

"I'm not escaping!" A bewildered little boy grabbed my
arm. "I told you my dad's got it all laid out."

"This is wrong, Luke. We're wrong, all wrong." I shook
my head. "Go home."

At around 4 P.M., he pulled me to him. "*You're* wrong,
Sophie." He kissed my hair over and over. "Maybe it didn't
start out that way, but I *do* love you. I love you so much."

I wanted to crawl into him.

"And you're right." He kissed my face, my eyes, kisses so
sweet they could crush you. And they did.

"You deserve better," he whispered.

I pushed him away at 4:05 P.M.

"Go."

Lucas Pearson shoved his hands into his pockets. A boy
with a heart full of hurt. He tried to smile, couldn't, so he
walked away. I watched him recede ever smaller, all the way
to the far end of the park's slope. Then Luke stopped and my

heart stopped with him. *Turn around. I take it back.* But he didn't. Luke Pearson never turned around; he just disappeared over the horizon.

My heart began beating again. Mary, Mother of God, it was cold.

But not too cold to cry.

Auntie Eva was wrong. I cried all the way home, not caring who I startled or alarmed.

I heard the music as soon as I got off on our floor. Nat King Cole was crooning up and over swelling violins and out into the hallway. "Autumn Leaves": not a good sign. Mama played that song over and over during the worst periods of Papa being in prison. I let myself in quietly and tiptoed over to her bedroom door. I couldn't hear crying, well, maybe just a little under Nat's velvety voice.

I should go in and check on her.

No. Whatever was going on between my mother and my father was between my mother and my father. It was enough that *I* had done the right thing. Luke, sweet Jesus, Luke. In my room, I lit my candle and made the sign of the cross. I could barely see the flicker through the blur of my tears. Dear God, Buddha, and Moses. If I did the righteous and good thing today, why in the name of all of you did it hurt so much?

I stumbled through the next few weeks, alternating between feeling fiercely righteous and hollowed out. One minute I was proud of myself for stepping away from starring in a soap opera, and the next I was twisting with certainty that no one would ever love me again. One minute I felt sorry for Luke, the next, I felt way, way sorrier for me. I switched back and forth from these extremes on a head-spinning ten-minute cycle. You had to pay attention to the cycle. The Blondes, for instance, never knew which me was going to turn up and say something over coffee at Mike's.

Yeah. I told them. All of it.

No one judged me. They were just there. I should have told all of them all of it right from the beginning. It's what I push them to do all the time. Secrets blossom with shame. No one knows that better than me. I prayed a lot. I prayed before I went to school and the moment I got back and before I went to bed. Mainly, I prayed for the hurt to stop. It seems that until it did, the Blondes had me under 24-hour surveillance. Either Sarah or Kit drove me home from school, and Madison called every single night. It was embarrassing and claustrophobic and pretty amazing.

"So, when all is said and done, it was a nothing," said Sarah, interrupting one of my cycles. "Basically an innocent nothing!" Sarah of all people was undertaking Blonde damage assessment and Sophie guilt management at Mike's. "It was a couple of kisses goodbye in a public park, right?"

"Right," I said. *Right?*

Dear Moses, that couldn't be right. It felt like so much more, all those weeks. It/he was so massive in my head, my heart, the guilt and the shame, but she was right. In terms of actual point-blank sinning, there were my thoughts and not much else. How could that be?

Wow.

There was a lot of hand patting and sympathetic nodding over the weeks, but mainly the Blondes were seriously relieved that Luke was gone. And shockingly, day by day, week by week, so was I. Eventually, it just got too hard to stay in that basement with Luke. It got more difficult to feel gutted about my choice to not go back to *their* apartment. Then I'd get a solid hit of that fierce righteous thing going. The virtuous bits got longer and longer. Still, every so often, out of the blue, I'd get punctured by the image of Luke, hands shoved in his pockets, walking away and not turning around.

And sweet Jesus that hurt. But less so each time.

The Blondes couldn't wait to redirect all their attention

away from Luke and onto the party. And so … somewhere in the middle of our costume fittings at Malabar, I actually got it. Somehow it dawned on me that this was *my* birthday, *my* party. It happened while we were looking to rent our poodle skirts. Poodle skirts were a fifties fashion staple. Massive fabric tenting and swinging out below the knees and cinched in tight at the waist with a shiny black belt. There is an actual poodle that is either appliquéd or embroidered onto each skirt. Kit was going to wear a powder-blue skirt and silk blouse with a Peter Pan collar, Sarah chose a lemon-yellow ensemble, and Madison picked out a baby-pink outfit. I reached for a pretty purple skirt, but Madison took my arm.

"No, sweetie, this is *your* party, and we are your handmaidens." Madison trotted to the front of the store and re-emerged with a large bundle of tissue paper. "*This* is your skirt." She pulled out a shiny black taffeta creation, which was held wide and flouncy by the acres of tulle fabric underneath it. A white silk poodle was embroidered on the front and white silk ruffles peeked out of the bottom of all that taffeta. It was gorgeous. Kit and Sarah beamed. You'd think they'd sewn it themselves.

"But?"

"And I took the liberty of buying you this dreamy white cashmere sweater as your birthday present. You can wear it after, for sure. Mummy got it at Creeds. It's a bit of heaven, if I do say so myself."

"Yeah, but, and thanks, but …"

"And we got the word out," said Kit. "No other girls can wear black and white, just the birthday girl."

"But …" My head was spinning. That the Blondes were bossy wasn't exactly a headline; that they were willing to fade into the background, at a party no less, was.

"Feel it," ordered Madison.

As soon as I touched the white cashmere, I was gone. It was like diving into the softest down-filled cloud. But way, way sexier.

"I'm in," I said and I meant it, not just about the party, but about my life too. I'd kept them all at arm's length all through the Luke thing. Enough. I had Blonde handmaidens, for God's sake! I wanted back into my life with my friends, back to us being *me and the Blondes*.

I had a party to star in.

We nixed saddle shoes in favour of black ballet flats and we bought pretty ruffled ankle socks. Mama arranged for Señora McClintock, Auntie Eva's Spanish-speaking hairdresser-cum-dress fitter, to do our hair for the big day. Since Mama had long run through her Mary Kay lipstick samples, she took us all to the Simpson's makeup department where we bought "big girl" lipsticks in various heart-stopping shades of red. A week before the party and in a moment of stupefying weakness, I agreed to get my ears pierced.

Kit bullied me into it. I had resisted getting my ears pierced my whole life. Given my colouring and hair, I was convinced earrings would make me look like a dime-store gypsy. Kit knew that.

"Buttercup, you're holding my life in your hands. I wouldn't steer you wrong. You were made for earrings."

"Speaking of life in hands …"

Kit groaned while the technician swabbed my earlobes with alcohol.

"Do you think you might want to tell them any time soon or …"

"I'm leaning toward the *or,*" she said.

"Oh." Little dots were marked on my earlobes. Apparently, my earlobes offended the Ukrainian technician. I had chubby earlobes.

"You okay with that?" Kit asked.

"Sure," I nodded, which only aggravated my Ukrainian earlobe person more. "It's your secret." What I really wanted was for her to tell so I could gauge everyone's reaction and sort out how this would come back on me. And, of course, on Kit too, and Lord knows I was burning up with a need to talk about the whole lesbian thing with somebody, anybody— really, absolutely anybody. I looked up at her. She was holding my hand, supposedly giving *me* courage. "I mean it, Kit. Only when you're ready."

"Thing is," she grasped on tighter while the Ukrainian loaded up her gun, "remember how Mike told you that lying about your old man in prison was just a 'place-holder' lie type of deal, until you, and the people around you, could deal with the truth?"

Damn. "Yeah, I remember," I muttered. "It meant a lot to me at the time. That he got it, I mean."

"I think I need some more place-holder time."

"Honestly, Kit, I get it." I nodded. And the Ukrainian slapped me. No kidding. She actually slapped my thigh.

"Don't move, already, or I vill put an earring in your forehead!"

I believed her.

We disinfected my ears every two hours for almost a week and then, on the day of my party, we stuck in sweet little seed pearl earrings. Kit was right—they looked amazing.

We were pretty giddy prepping at Auntie Eva's on the day of the party. That's right *day*. It took hours. The Señora decided the only way to go was with very high, structured ponytails. The Blondes were pulled and yanked and tied while their ponytails were fashioned into one long sausage curl. It was quite a process trying to tame my hair into smooth slick order, but she did it, and then she let my curls go wild in the tail bit. No pain, no gain was our mantra. All of us got singed at least once by the curling iron, but the Señora was a miracle worker. When I saw them, Kit, Sarah, and Madison all done up, my heart lurched—they were that beautiful. My Blondes. "You all look like Sandra Dee in *Gidget*. What I wouldn't give to—"

Madison grabbed my arms and spun me around to face the full-length mirror. "To look exactly like you do, Sophie. Look! Just look at you!"

"Wow." Kit came up and whispered in my ear, "I take back what I said before. I defy *anyone* of any inclination not to find you irresistible."

"He'll melt," said Sarah.

"Who?" I asked

But Mama and the Aunties blew in like tornadoes. "Chop, chop, let's go!" Auntie Radmila teared up when she saw me. "Your Papa iz down the stairs vit za stretchy car. *Yoy!*" She pinched my cheek. "Even more too beautiful zen your Mama vas on za night she met your Papa!"

"Qvik, qvik!" Auntie Eva waved at us.

"Vait, vait, vait!" Mama fumbled around until she retrieved Papa's old camera.

All urgency was swept aside. We spent the next twenty minutes in every possible pose and combination until Papa came bounding up the stairs. Mama gasped when she saw him. He wore an old-fashioned black tux, the kind with the shiny stripe down the legs, and a blindingly white accordion-pleated shirt. He looked like he should be on a stage somewhere. Mama floated over to him and carefully pinned a white carnation into his lapel. I knew in my bone marrow that she would have held that moment for many beats longer, but Papa stuck to the task of hustling us along. "Ladies?! Let's go, ladies!" He clapped his hands until he saw me. Papa strode right over, took my hand, and twirled me around and around. "There will be no one else in the room but you," he whispered. "Tonight is your night, Sophia. You deserve it." He kissed the top of my head. Mama clicked.

And I will keep that photo forever.

22

Mike's was unrecognizable. Hell, Mike was unrecognizable. He wore a white sport coat and powder-blue ruffled shirt that Auntie Luba rented from Mr. Big 'N Tall. He looked almost as handsome as he did on his wedding day. The restaurant was transformed. The whole place was smothered in pink and white carnations, either the actual flowers or the handcrafted tissue paper variety that you see festooned on bridal limousines, thousands and thousands of them. They made the restaurant look silly and pretty and sweet all at once.

"You like?" asked Auntie Eva.

"Like? I love!" I hugged her. "Love, love, love! But how did they talk you into this? I know you hate carnations."

Auntie Radmila waved her hand. "Pshaw! It vas her idea."

"Oooh Lordy, it's magic!" gushed Sarah.

Auntie Luba pointed out that even the Hamilton blender

was covered in carnations. "Ve made one hundred and fifty-two tousand million."

Auntie Radmila pulled Madison and me into her. "I haven't seen Eva so happy since before za funeral, I tell you true, Sophie." She patted her chest lovingly. "You are for sure having a Sveet Seventeen for all of us." Her eyes threatened to well up and my eyes threatened to join them.

"Oh no you don't!" Madison fanned her hand in front of my face furiously. "No crying! You have mascara on, Sophie. And no eating either, you're wearing scarlet-red lipstick that will bleed all over the place. You can't risk it!"

Auntie Radmila looked at Madison like she'd never seen her before. She reached up and cupped Madison's chin in her hand. "Zer must be some Slavic in you, my child!"

"Attago, Madison," I said. "There is no greater Auntie compliment."

"Oh go on." She rolled her eyes but still gave Auntie Radmila an extra peck on the cheek before linking her arm through mine. "Let's check out the dance floor."

The back of Mike's, the dancing area per se, was washed in a cool darkness. The rear of the restaurant had been cleared of tables. While the front was fun and pretty and covered in carnations, back here it was inky and waiting for whispers. A few chairs were placed against the walls in little groupings and the only lighting came off the glow of the jukebox, which flashed different colours and intensity depending on the song. Mike had it restocked with fifties tunes and it would continue to play just with buttons—no quarters necessary. The ceiling was covered with miles of twirling pink and white paper streamers captured by a big pink heart in the centre, making it feel like we were in a private tent.

"Oh my!" I said to no one.

"Buboola!" I heard Auntie Eva's unmistakable bellow. "Come up to za front to greeting your guests."

It was 9:05. The invitation said 9 P.M. Platters of munchies covered every surface. Mike and a Macedonian woman who worked as a caterer would be staying the whole time, getting drinks for people who more or less looked the legal age of eighteen and soft drinks for everyone else.

9:09.

No one would come. Mama asked whether I was having fun. I looked at her anxious face and swallowed my percolating anxiety. "Are you kidding, Mama? It's all beyond brilliant. I'm out of my head with happiness." She took a picture.

9:14.

"Okay, well, that's it, might as well call it a day," I said. Everybody pretended not to hear me.

9:19.

"Seriously."

And then they came. They came in groups of six or so. Not only did they come, but they came dressed to perfection, bearing balloons and flowers and gifts.

For me.

I was so relieved and stunned that I almost started crying again. Madison pinched the back of my arm and rescued me from mascara destruction. The girls wore various versions of poodle skirts, or jeans rolled up to mid-calf with tucked-in checked shirts, or in form-fitting pencil skirts and skin-tight sweaters with little silk kerchiefs tied around their necks that made them look adult and knowing. I couldn't help but notice that most of the girls that David had romanced were in the skin-tight category. I felt eleven whenever I looked at them.

"Who invited them?" I whined to Kit, who looked over and shrugged.

"Shit happens," she said helpfully.

The boys, not to be outdone, were also dressed to kill. No ratty bell-bottoms here. Straight-leg jeans and varsity jackets over snowy-white shirts were the norm. But some of the boys wore beautiful narrow suits and skinny ties. Other boys wore cuffed jeans and skin-tight white T's. They were Brylcreemed within an inch of their lives. Paul Wexler came in one of those beautiful suits and presented me with a wrist corsage. "A beautiful orchid for a beautiful birthday girl." He slid it on my wrist. Auntie Eva stepped closer to observe this and examine him.

"Thank you so much, Paul." I stood on my tiptoes and kissed him on the cheek. "It's beautiful!" If I put some real effort into it, I bet I could totally warm up to him.

"You owe me a dance, Sophie, and I intend to claim it this time."

"Sure thing," I said at the same time that Auntie Eva "harrumphed."

The jukebox started up. The Blondes were in high flirt mode, with Mike Jr. and George hot on the heels of Madison and Sarah. I know Mike was counting on the cousins to act as bouncers, if need be. Good luck with that. Those boys were not in bouncer mode. I caught Mike Jr. dragging Madison to the back of the restaurant. He actually got her onto the dance floor and kept her there, even though they were the only couple dancing. Unbelievable.

The place was filling up fast. I was dizzy from being kissed, hugged, passed around, and propelled from person to person. Between the music and the din of people, it was hard to hear, still, I couldn't help but catch Auntie Eva and Auntie Luba's simultaneous cry of *"Yoy!"* when David stepped through the door.

All by himself.

Straight black jeans, snug, very snug, faded black T-shirt, and a well-worn, soft, black leather jacket. Jesus. Auntie Eva looked like she was going to faint. "Behave!" I warned through clenched teeth. I don't know who I was warning. I mean, sweet Moses, it was an extremely flattering, um, look. Every muscle was defined and highlighted on all six-foot-four of him. Like the other boys, David had Brylcreemed his hair; unlike the other boys he knew to use just "a little dab." David's thick dark hair still fell into his eyes. He had to keep pushing it back with his hand.

Danger, Sophie Kandinsky, danger.

And all this with just one foot into the restaurant!

When he got to us, David reached for Auntie Luba's then Auntie Eva's hands and told them what a pleasure it was to see them again. I felt a powerful breeze from the massive eyelash fluttering beside me. He must have thought he was standing in a wind tunnel.

If you tilted your head, just so, you could actually see the outline of his stomach muscles underneath the shirt. Just when he moved in a certain way mind you, like reaching for an Auntie's hand, and then only if you strained. The Aunties were straining. Hell, I was straining. That was the trouble; he must be so aware of the effect he has on … much older women. I made a concerted attempt at a normal welcoming smile. I was furious with all of them.

"Happy birthday, Sophie. You look like a dream." David reached for my hand and brought it near his mouth, held it there for a heartbeat and then gently, tenderly, brushed the front of my fingers with his lips. Then he eyed my wrist corsage and frowned. "Oh no, not tonight. No more." He slid the corsage off my wrist with one hand before I even knew what was happening. It felt like he was undressing me.

I came out of my fog long enough to protest. "Now wait a gosh-darned minute, David. Paul Wexler just …" Really, was that the best I could do?! *Gosh-darned?* I was appalled with myself. Meanwhile, David asked permission to put the orchid on Auntie Eva who had to steady herself on Auntie Radmila. Won't that just make Paul's day. When Auntie Radmila stopped giggling, David reached behind Mike's cash register and opened a little cellophane box. It was another wrist corsage. I had to think hard about my mascara. The corsage was a very sweet, very old-fashioned arrangement of pink and white carnations set in baby's breath. David slid his corsage on my wrist like he'd been born and raised to do nothing but that. Auntie Eva grabbed my other hand. "There," he said, smiling at my hand, "much better," and then at me. "You may be an orchid, Sophie, but I know you *love* carnations. I remember your Aunt teasing you about it."

"Ow!" Auntie Eva dug her nails into my hand like she was searching for an artery. I didn't think she could take much more of this. "Thank you, David." I looked around and behind him for his date, his entourage. He never roamed loose. Sure enough, a few girls were waving at him from one of the back booths. "It's, they're perfect."

He leaned in closer to me. "I won't claim the first dance since you've probably got that reserved for your father, but will you promise me the one after that?"

"Absolutely, *pa da,* for sure, she does!"

"Auntie Radmila!"

David smiled, both dimples fully engaged. His black eyes lit me up. "Good, I'll come for you then." We watched him walk away, melt into the crowd, into his friends. We, Auntie Eva, Auntie Luba, Auntie Radmila, and Sarah, who had just joined us, sighed.

"Wow, James Dean and Elvis rolled into one." Sarah thrust a lipstick at me. "Madison said freshen up your lips and not to worry. The entire second string is going to double-team him while you do your hostess-like thing. Those girls won't get anywhere near him tonight!"

"Really," I said. "What for? Why would I care? Who cares? Why does no one care that I don't care?" I stroked my carnations. It felt like someone had injected a syringe of caffeine straight into my heart. What was the matter with me?

Auntie Luba and Sarah rolled their eyes at the same time.

"Lipstick!" ordered Auntie Eva. She looked around and then grabbed both of my arms. "Zat von." She indicated with her head to the back of the room where David was horsing around with Stewart Morgan and Kyle Levy. My heart galloped as soon as I caught sight of him. "Your Mama vould not saying zis to you because it vould be in a property."

It took me a second. "Do you mean inappropriate?"

"*Zat* is vat I said," she said. "Za point is, you are afraid."

I opened my mouth to deny it but was greeted by three new people coming in before being hijacked by Auntie Eva again. She was like a dog with a bone. "You are seventeen, Sophie. Don't be afraid. And don't be afraid of zat von." Again with the head pointing. "Za boy is a shotgun, but he is yours, eh." I made a face. "Iz true. I love you and your pieces, but don't be an idiot, Sophie!"

I watched as Jennifer Giacometti tried to pull David onto the dance floor. He wasn't having it. David? *Mine?* I saw two of our second string make their way over to him to run interference.

I nodded. "Auntie Eva?"

"Yes, buboola?"

"I, well, I know we, you all, had agreed that you, the adults, I mean, except for Mike of course, anyway, you said that you would leave by midnight and …"

"Vat midnight?" She looked at her watch. It was 10:10. "I could barely not make it to eleven o'clock even, eh, Luba?"

Luba frowned and then nodded and threw in a yawn for good effect. "I am so tired, I cannot be standing anozer minute even. I hope you don't mind?"

"*Da!*" Auntie Eva had to shout above the din. "Sorry, sorry, but ve, za old people, have to going home in a few minutes, not a minute more. I vill go right now and remind your Papa and Mama how tired zey are."

I threw my arms around her. "I love you, Auntie Eva!"

"Of course you do, buboola." She pinched my cheek. "You love me because you are zat fantastik *and* I am zat fantastik."

And right then and there, at 10:12 P.M., Saturday, February 17, 1977, I believed her on both counts.

Mama asked whether I was having fun. As soon as I assured her that I was, she took my picture, again. It was like she needed every happy breath recorded for future proof. Finally, Papa came to the rescue. He took my hand and led me onto the dance floor in one long and fluid movement. I blew thank-you kisses to Mama and the Aunties the whole way. "So, we old folks are all exhausted, eh?" Papa winked. "So tired in fact that we must leave immediately?"

"Yes, Papa, it really is a pity. But don't feel bad. I understand and I'm sure you can still find enough energy for one quick dance with Mama."

Papa shook his head. "No, Princess, tonight is *your* night and yours alone." He kissed my forehead and then looked around the crowded room and crowded dance floor as we waited for the next song to come on. "Which one is he, Sophie?"

"I don't know what you mean." The jukebox delivered "My Special Angel" by Bobbie Helms.

Papa rolled his eyes, or the grown-up version of it. "Let's not go through that again, Sophie. Every time we dance, you're trying to hide a boy from me."

I winced. He was right. The last time we danced was at Mike and Auntie Luba's wedding, just before Luke and I snuck out on the landing together, before Luke knew about Alison, before so much and so long ago.

"He's behind you, black T-shirt." Papa started to turn. "Don't look!" He waited three heartbeats and then twirled me just as the chorus hit. Very smooth my Papa is.

"Your coach?" he said, trying not to look unnerved.

"Assistant coach," I corrected.

"Ah, I see." Papa was quiet as he whirled me around the dance floor. The other couples stopped to watch us. No one is a better dancer than my father. "Sophie," Papa whispered, "I was still sick, I mean, I was drinking last year when your heart was trampled on. I caused you pain when you were already hurting." Luke again. "And I missed your life even when I was in the middle of it."

I began to deny it, but Papa shushed me.

"But, I believe, I understand from your Mama that you were not abused in the process."

"Abused? Luke?" I sighed. "No, Papa, in the end, too much had already happened for anything like that to happen."

"Pardon?"

"Don't worry." I shook my head. "Nothing happened that a father has to worry about, I swear."

He took in David. "I'm sober now, Sophie. You are a year older and with every year in life and love, the stakes are higher." Papa crooked his finger under my chin and smiled. "If he hurts you, I will kill him."

I stood on my tiptoes and kissed his rough cheek. "I'll be sure to tell him, Papa, but it may not come up. It's pretty confusing all in all. He seems to be angry with me more than anything else. I don't have a clue as to what his real feelings are."

Papa raised my hand with the carnation corsage. "I do," he sighed. "That young man has not taken his eyes off you since he walked in the door."

"Oh Papa!"

"Don't you 'oh Papa,' me. Fathers know about these things. I am on alert, Sophie, and this time, I will stay on alert."

And then I got it. He was trying so hard. Papa needed me to know he was watching and that he was here this time. "I know, Papa. Glad to have you back."

He squeezed my hand. "My special birthday present to you will be ready next Saturday at 4 P.M. Reserve the date for your old man, will you?"

"Of course, Papa. And we'll save all you old people some birthday cake!" As soon as the song was over, Papa stood ready to go, but instead of leading me off the dance floor, he waited.

I felt him in waves breaking behind me.

"Good evening, Mr. Kandinsky."

Papa nodded. "David."

"May I have the honour of the next dance with the birthday girl, sir?"

Papa looked at David, David looked at me, and the whole floor, including the girls in the tight skirts, looked at us.

Papa leaned over and kissed my forehead. "Happy birthday, Princessa." Then he placed my hand onto David's. David gave him a little nod. And my father walked away.

David stepped in front of me. "Sophie." Oh my. All I could see was him. Well technically, just his chest, his shoulders, and his arms, those arms, *what arms*. I moved my head up a fraction, his jaw was clenched, and his mouth, uh … I levelled my gaze back down to his chest. My right hand was still placed flat against David's open palm. My hand is cold. His hand is warm and large but not rough. I'm surprised by this. Instead of clasping my hand, David slides his palm over to the outside of my hand, covering it. I'm surprised by this too. He locks on, turns my hand into him, and then pulls my palm flat to the centre of his chest.

Jesus.

A surge of electricity rushes from him right through to me.

I didn't have a chance.

The lights dim even further. The adults were gone. Bobby Darin comes on with "Dream Lover." It's a night of Bobbies, Bobbie Helms and now Bobby Darin. There are no Bobbies now. Where did all the Bobbies go, I wonder, trying to maintain focus, but I can't. I can't because my hand is on his perfectly carved beating chest. I realize with a shock that my heart is pounding in rhythm with his. Maybe it always did.

I raised my left arm and placed it on top of David's shoulder and behind his neck. The underside of my arm was alive to every nuance of his movement. Each time his body stirred, the soft part of my arm sensed his muscles and sinews reacting and anticipating the actual motion. It was not possible that I felt the things that I did just dancing.

Hello, I was in trouble here, and we hadn't even gotten to the chorus.

David covered the small of my back with his left hand and with no discernible effort at all, pulled me to him, hard. Of all the things I felt in that one delirious moment, the most stunning was that *I am safe*.

David looked down at me, his hair falling into his eyes. I went to brush it away, but he stopped me. He intertwined his fingers into mine, brought my hand up to his mouth and kissed the back of my fingers, tasting each one. Stuff was firing from places I didn't even know could fire. My entire Sweet Seventeen self lit up with sparklers. This couldn't be right. Then he laid my hand flat against his heart again, pressing it deeper into the soft, thin fabric, covering it with his hand. David's heart beat through my fingers, into me, and straight through to my heart. The drumming within me was deafening.

"You feel so right, Sophie." He caressed my back, running his hand up and then back down, pressing me to him.

"It's the sweater," I said because I am a blue ribbon idiot. All I wanted to do was wrap my legs around him and then … well, okay, then it got a little fuzzy, but clearly, I needed kissing, if nothing else to shut me up. "It's *real* cashmere." I sounded like I was starring in a Florida orange juice commercial. "Isn't it amazing?" It was official: my mouth was running amok. I never knew what that meant until that exact moment when I was amokking all over the place. "I've been feeling myself all day." Aargh! Holy Moses, kill me or kiss me, but somebody shut me up!

"Hmm …" He bent down and growled in my ear while he travelled the breadth of my back with his hand before settling just below my waist again. "Hmm. No, not the sweater. You."

David moved me around the floor with his thigh. It took every ounce of concentration in me to not think about that. With what was left, I tried to anticipate his touch. And couldn't. It was a shock each time he caressed me. When his thumb stroked the curve of my back, I dissolved.

"How are you feeling, birthday girl?" he whispered, grazing my ear with his lips.

"Overstimulated," I chirped. Dear God, find a stick and beat me silent! If he didn't kiss me pronto, I'd ruin everything.

Instead, David threw his head back and laughed! Madison and Mike Jr. were dancing beside us. They looked over and smiled. So did Sarah and George. I probably smiled back, but all I wanted was to crawl into David's beating black T-shirt.

"Sophie, Sophie." David shook his head and took me into him again. Ahhh, I exhaled into his chest. He let go of the top of my hand just long enough to raise my chin. "There's nobody like you, and I knew that the minute I first saw you when you were in grade nine." Whoa. What? I was getting confused. I needed kissing in the worst way. Instead he wrapped his arms around me. "I saw you first. I need you to know that. I should've told you sooner." He kissed my hair. "Much sooner. I've waited long enough and tonight, I'm hoping we can start like we should have two years ago."

My head spun. Wait, wait. Even in my highly flammable state, I sensed that this was something. That he was saying stuff. "What do you mean, you *saw* me *first*? What do you mean grade nine?" David pressed my hand back onto his chest. Damn. I mean, oh my God, what was I supposed to do with all of that at my fingertips? I forgot the questions. Didn't care about the answers.

· He drew in his breath, which was a beautiful thing to experience with my hands on him. The boy smelled like Ivory soap and … me.

"Yeah." He smiled. "So, a couple of years ago, I was bored and I checked out the girls' junior tryouts." My face burned. I had an instant cringing recall of trying so hard to impress the Blondes, to make them like me, accept me, and protect me, all in one lousy basketball tryout.

"You lit up the floorboards. Not only were you better than anyone had a right to be on a junior court, but the way you looked, moved, smiled … it was ridiculous. I was gone, lost to a kid that was all curls and fire. You were, you *are* like nobody else."

"But …" I suddenly remembered him and Luke at practices, at a couple of our games, and at Mike's on Saturdays. David had always hung back. I saw that now. David had stayed away. "Then why …?"

He put a finger to my mouth.

"Like an ass, I even pointed you out to Luke." The muscles underneath his skin tensed and held. "We, we were competitive then."

"No." *David's always been jealous of me. If he knew about*

you … Luke's body language, the way he looked away when he had said that. I knew even then when he tried to sell it to me that day at the park.

"He baited me about you, but I wouldn't bite. You were too young, Sophie, I couldn't …"

Luke had lied.

"Much too young," David whispered.

What the …? "Hey, you're only two years older than me!" He pulled my fingers to his mouth. Bit. Dear God.

"There are lots of ways of being too young."

David cupped my face and then moved me so that he could kiss below my ear and then planted soft little butterfly kisses beside my eye until I just about passed out. "And you're still too young, Sophie Kandinsky. It's just that I can't wait anymore, and I will not risk you getting involved with another fool."

Wait, wait. "So, was I like a game to Luke?"

I felt, rather than saw, his jaw twitch. "Maybe, in the beginning." He grazed my ear again, whispering. "See, I wasn't watching out for him—he had Alison. I thought she kept him busy enough. I was wrong. I should've paid attention. I should have …" David placed my head back against his chest. "I don't believe you stayed a game to him, Sophie." His body tightened. "But I'll admit that I thought long and hard about lying to you about that."

Oh, Luke. I burned up tears before they could form.

The song ended. Neither of us moved or breathed until the next one came on, Elvis's "Love Me Tender."

"Sophie?"

It felt true, all of it. "You don't need the lie, David." I skimmed his shoulder, the nape of his neck, reaching for him.

"It made me crazy, the whole thing, him." He paused. "Him and you. I wanted to kill him. Luke treated Alison like a joke, but at least he manned up and married her when he had to. I was sorry, but I was relieved too, relieved he'd stay away from you." David kissed my eyes and then folded me into him again. "But even with him married, I couldn't be sure he'd stay away. He knew I was still gone on you. Then, when I saw him at the funeral." His back stiffened. "He was after you again. I was so pissed, I couldn't see straight for weeks wondering if you were meeting, where, how … Sophie, I was such a jerk. See, every time I saw you, I'd see him and you. Forgive me." He nuzzled my neck. "Can we start again?" He kissed my throat. "Please give me a chance." My entire body agreed, no contest.

His voice was low and rough. "Hi, my name is David. I play basketball. I've got a big game next week. Would you like to come?" He'd kiss me if I nodded.

I nodded.

David kissed my earlobe and then bit. My head exploded. Would he kiss me now? "Then since I can't risk you getting mixed up with other unsavoury types," he squinted into the darkness and surveyed the room until he zeroed in on Paul, "would you consider coming as my girl? I think I've waited long enough, don't you?"

David took my face into his hands. He kissed my eyes. "Say yes, David." How could I be so alert and so hypnotized at the same time? His face, his mouth was an inch from mine. "Yes,

David!" And then I was seized by panic. The boy had a cast of thousands. "Wait, what does that mean, 'your girl' exactly?"

"It means," he kissed my forehead, "that you are mine," kissed my cheek, "and I, Sophie Kandinsky, am …" kissed the top of my chest, "so yours." Then finally, finally, David nudged my mouth open with his and I fell into him, ready or not. It was a hard, hungry kiss that went on forever and nowhere near long enough. No gentleness for either of us. Bits of me, the bits that were locked up and careful, concerned with image, and consumed with being safe, all those bits broke off and fell to the floor in that kiss.

The song ended. David pulled away. And I swear to God, it hurt.

Even in the semi-dark, I could tell there was a crowd around us.

"Holy Hannah!" yelled Kit above the din. "Talk about combustible!" It was true. I was going to be able to light my birthday candles just by standing next to them.

Sarah squeezed my arm.

"Okay, that's enough cheap physical stuff. There's a birthday cake to eat." Madison pulled me forward to the front of the restaurant.

David placed one hand at the small of my back, protectively. He leaned over to me and whispered, "What would you like to do, Sophie?"

Kiss some more was probably not the right answer, but there wasn't an inch of me that wasn't vibrating like a tuning fork. "Cake is good," I squeaked.

"Cake it is!"

My team made way in front of us to reveal a monster slab of chocolate fudge birthday cake lit with seventeen pink candles and one white one for good luck. David stood behind me. Mike handed me a shot glass of brandy and poured one for himself. The rest of the room sang "Happy Birthday," including, albeit grudgingly, all the girls in the tight skirts. Mike clinked our shot glasses. "On behalf of your Mama and Papa and your Aunties and …" He raised his glass to Kit, to Madison, to Sarah, and then, finally to David. "Know that you are loved, on this your seventeenth birthday. *Živili,* Sophia Kandinsky."

"Thank you, Mike." I raised my glass first to him and then the rest of the room. "Thank you all so much for all of this! I'm the luckiest Sweet Seventeen on the planet!"

We downed our shots and everybody clapped, for a long time.

I clapped too. My cheeks hurt from smiling so hard.

David reached down behind me, kissed the nape of my neck so tenderly that I was sent flying again. "Go on," he said. Tonight, I was invincible, almost. A bullet of ice-cold fear shot through me. Dear God and everybody at home on my little altar, wasn't it against the rules for someone like me to be this happy? Surely, I would have to pay? Then I blew out every single one of my birthday candles. David kissed me again, and it didn't matter. Even if I did, tonight was worth it. Whatever the price.

24

I wore his kisses for days. I wore them sleeping, bathing, washing dishes, and going to school. Every so often, like in the middle of math class, they'd make me shiver uncontrollably, but I still wore them. *You are mine and I am yours.* I could call up and relive his touch so clearly that it felt like everybody in the room could see his hands on me. It made me crazed, but it was also serious proof that my birthday happened the way I thought it happened. Didn't it?

But I knew it did, because I confirmed it the very next day when Madison came over for the official party debriefing. I talked about it and David, smiling non-stop. So *this* was what *that* was all about. I finally got it. I let Madison say three or four words about her and Mike Jr., about Sarah and George, about the other couples, and even a few words about Kit and "poor, poor lovelorn Rick," but then it would be right back to David and me. Didn't that have a pretty ring to it? *David and me.* Madison pretended she didn't mind; after all, Mike Jr. was like her hundredth boyfriend and David was my first … real one.

I had a boyfriend.

Maybe it wasn't a dream.

But it sure felt like one.

Things like this don't happen to people like me.

Then Madison would tell me over and over again that they could and they did. She whispered it over Hungarian goulash when Mama was in the room, and she said it much louder in my room. "Things like that can happen to you, Sophie Kandinsky. He is crazy about you. He was pretty clear about that." She also said that the whole thing had pumped her up something fierce. "I'm going to tell them, Soph."

"Who, what?"

"Kit and Sarah, about crazy Edna being my real grandmother."

"Really, for sure?"

"Yup, I've already told Edna that I'm going to straighten it all out."

"Wow, she must be over the moon," I said.

"Yeah, she was bawling and tooting all over the place this afternoon. I think she'll be really happy not to be introduced as our former cleaning lady anymore." Madison picked up my Buddha and put him down like he was red hot. "I'm ashamed of that, Soph."

"Hell, we've all got stuff, Madison!" I thought about almost going over the edge with Luke, about Sarah struggling to stay a born-again virgin, and about Kit struggling as to whether she should come out or not. "In fact, your stuff is pretty tame compared with most of us." She almost smiled. "You're royalty, Madison. We know it and you know it. Edna's not going to change that."

"Oh, Sophie."

"Yeah, yeah, but enough about you. Let's get back to David and me!"

That's how I kept his kisses warm, right up until David's basketball game on Thursday. I blathered on about him non-stop, and to their eternal credit, Madison, Kit, and Sarah listened non-stop.

I had a boyfriend.

Hey, not only did I have a boyfriend, I had this miracle boy who jumped out of stairwells to hug me. Who searched for me at lunch, who lived leaning against my locker before his practices, and who showed me off to his friends. No more skulking around, worried who might see. If I caught his voice in the hallway, my heart would pitch and roll. So would his. I know because he would place my hand on it and then cover it with his.

Kit came with me to the game. Madison and Sarah were having an early dinner at Edna's. It was secret-sharing time. The deal was that Madison would fess up that Edna was actually her grandmother on the way there, and if she didn't, Edna would do it herself over dinner. Madison designed it so that she'd have no wiggle room. It worked and we knew this because she did the exact same thing with Kit the day before.

"And … so?" I asked while keeping an eye on David running his layups before the whistle.

"And so what?" shrugged Kit. "Loony-tune Edna is Madison's biological grandmother. I mean *really,* so what? Madison was so tortured you'd think she was revealing something that was going to undermine the fate of the free world."

He moved with superb power and speed. The men's game was completely different from ours. It was brutal. I tried to brace myself for what was coming. "Thing is," I turned back to Kit, "it was taking up a lot of messy space in her head all this time." I planted my face in front of hers. "Secrets will do that."

She pushed my head out of her line of sight. The teams were whistled off and whistled on. Northern was playing Central Collegiate. We had a nice crowd for our boys since it was close to playoffs. They lined up for the toss. David was captain and right forward. The ball was tossed. He got it and off we went.

"Wow, he *is* something to look at." She shook her head. "I swear if anyone could turn me—"

I jabbed her.

"Hey, keep your elbows to yourself! I'm kidding! Sort of." We were first on the board. While she was still clapping, Kit turned to me. "I just can't, you know? I thought about it a million ways since we last talked. They're not ready." Kit looked around; we still had a lot of room around us. She turned back to the court. "And I'm not ready *and* I'm gutless. Hell, I haven't even been able to tell my mom that I'm not coming next year."

"Kit, that's so not true. The gutless part, I mean." The ball sped up and down and up the floor, sprouting baskets at each end. Then Central started laying on the muscle. "I don't get it. You're the most courageous of all of us."

"Uh, no …" Her eyes stayed glued to the play. "That would be you, Sophie. I make a lot of noise, but like I say, gutless. I can't believe that *you,* of all people, bought it. I hate confrontation and inconvenient personal honesty."

David was elbowed on the way down from a layup. The ref missed it, but David didn't. They were now up by two. "Okay maybe, but your mom …"

"Look, I will for sure tell my mom soon." Her shoulders slumped. "And the rest of them … about the rest of it … later."

"That's cool." I looked at her. "Like I said before, I get it."

"Besides, I'm doing it for you. You'd be lost if you weren't holding anyone's secrets! I can't imagine Sophie secretless."

I smiled remembering Sarah and our trip to Honest Ed's.

"Uh-uh." She shook her head. "I know what you're thinking, but sweet Sarah coughed up about your adventures in condom-land the night of your party."

It was 24 to 18 for us. David sank two shots from a personal foul and they were on him hard.

"Really?" I said.

"Yup. Not only that, but she says that she's not going to open up that box of safes. It seems like our girl is determined to stick to her new-found purity after all."

I bit my tongue.

"Yeah," she sighed. "I don't buy it either, but you can't deny that she totally means it in the moment."

It was 31 to 30 at the end of the first quarter, and David was responsible for nine of those points. He had blistering control and the welts to show for it. David gave as good as he got. I never realized just how loud the men's game was. The sounds of violence pierced me, a grunt before a shove, skin on skin, muscle pushing against bone, shoes squealing on the floor. Central was taking cheap shots at David. He wouldn't last into the second half at this rate. My stomach knotted as he loped over to the free-throw line.

"Sweet Sarah." I shook my head. "I've said it before, but if the rest of the school knew just how screwed up we are, they'd charge admission."

"Oh, that's only us individually." Kit threw her arm around my neck. "Together we're indestructible. Hell, together we're immortal, don't you think?"

"I *think* you're demented," I said.

The gym doors swung open and heads turned for Anita Shepard, Janice Wilton, and a few more of David's special "fans." Janice wore a tight paisley-patterned mini-dress with shiny black boots. The paisleys hugged and swirled around her body in a way guaranteed to make every boy dizzy.

I sucked in some air and felt eleven all over again.

"Steady, girl," whispered Kit.

David made a shot from the top of the key. He looked for me and winked before he jogged back up the court.

I exhaled.

"Speaking of virginity," Kit said.

"We weren't."

"Yeah we were, Sarah's on again, off again virginity. What are *you* going to do, Soph? You are not Sarah."

No use pretending I didn't know what she meant. I looked

back at Janice and the air leaked out of me. "I've been praying to my altar about it."

"And?" She moved in closer and handed me her Pot O' Gloss. "Start smearing. It's your best coping technique."

I applied lip gloss like it was going to win the game for us. "I don't think I'm ready, Kit." David reached for a long jump and made it. What arms, those amazing arms. A boy could hold up the world with arms like that. "But the way he makes me feel … I'm … it scares me. It's like my skin's on too tight, but still, I'm not really, entirely, ready for *that,* not yet."

"Tell him," she said. "I mean it. Straight up. Don't mess this up, Sophie, you guys were meant for each other. Don't play games. Tell him or you'll lose your courage and pretend you're ready when you're not. *Don't* pretend you're something when you're not."

"Like *you,* you mean?" I wanted to suck the words back instantly. "I am a worm and must be crushed. Sorry, sorry."

"You're right." Kit looked down at her hands. "I know about the not having courage part. About the not being true to yourself part." Then she smiled. "Maybe I need you to be my role model, eh?"

"He'll dump me," I whined. "Why wouldn't he? I'd dump me. I mean, he has had …" I snuck a look at Janice, Anita, and the others. There were so many others. "Let's face it, he makes Luke look like a boy scout."

"Yeah, but he's smarter than Luke." Kit snatched her lip gloss back. "Look, that boy has cut a wide swath through this school while he was waiting for you, no doubt about it. I think we're pretty well the only ones he hasn't slept with."

I groaned.

"*Sophie,* none of them is his girl. *You* are. He made that pretty public at your party. I'm dead serious about this. Don't pretend. Pretending sucks. Massive mistake."

"Whoa, Kit, 'fear of confrontation' my foot!"

She rolled her eyes, just as Janice and the girls began cheering extra exuberantly. Bouncing up and down like that, they made the cheerleaders look like Mennonites. A few guys from our chemistry class and a couple of football players came in and joined Kit and me, beefing up our cheering section but putting an end to our heart to heart. Just as well. I was in a righteous freakout as it was.

At the top of the fourth quarter, David was nailed coming down from a jump shot just inside the key. Number 34 elbowed him in the cheek, just missing his eye. David started bleeding immediately. I exploded out of my seat and would've leapt onto the court if it weren't for the quick hands of Kit and Joshua Singer.

"What are you going to add to the party?" Kit patted my knee. "His people will take care of it."

And so they did. While David was getting patched up, his right guard and left forward double-teamed 34, sent him flying, and stepped on his hand by accident as he tried to get up. He had to leave the game. Message delivered. No fouls.

"Told ya!" said Kit.

So this was how the big boys played.

We won 67 to 59. Kit wouldn't let me wait outside the boys' locker room by myself. Thank God, since as soon as we turned the corner we saw Janice Wilton, panting outside the doors. Kit glared at her. Janice took off as soon as we parked ourselves across the hall from the doorway and made it clear we weren't moving. We watched Janice wiggle away. "*Your* people will take care of that," said Kit. "One of us will always be with you on slut alert after each game."

The boys broke through the doors hooting and hollering, smelling like Irish Spring and victory. We got a lot of long looks and low wolf whistles.

David beamed as soon as he caught sight of us. "Hey, Kit, thanks for coming and thanks for taking care of my girl here." He winked at her. "Let us walk you home."

"Damn, and manners too! I swear, Soph, he *could* turn me." She walked off down the hall. "Thanks, but I've got my car," she called.

"Turn her?"

"Never mind." I pulled his head toward me, stood on my tip-toes, and ever so gently kissed the surgical tape on his cheek. "You were awesome, a machine, amazing, terrifying …"

"What's wrong, Sophie?"

David dropped his gym bag and leaned back into the lockers. He put his hands on my waist and pulled me in a bit. I instantly started to pulse. My body was built for cheap romance novels. "See!" I said accusingly. "See!"

"Uh … no." He smiled.

I sighed for extra courage. David waited patiently, looking at me and looking amused. I wanted to remember how sweet he was right then, all clean and scrubbed, his hair still wet, and wearing a little white bandage high on his cheekbone. His mouth curled up into a smile, anticipating something. I photographed him in my head, my heart imprinting every part of him. It had been a miraculous five days.

"All you do is touch me and I lose it!"

His eyes danced and he gripped me tighter. "That's bad?" he asked.

"Aargh!" I looked at the ceiling, examining the acoustic tiles. Then I faced him with my heart firmly planted in my feet. "David, you don't know what you do to me. You may think you do, but you don't, not really, because you're not me, thing is, I'm so incredibly … but, you said yourself that there were lots of ways of being too young, and Anita and Janice and Susan and God knows how many others were not too young that way so that you must be used to getting … of course and why not, but I just can't because I'm not like Alison, but then if you asked my body, I am, but on the other hand you know, maybe the religion stuff got to me after all at least for now, the next little while, I mean, you know?" I looked deep into his eyes and got lost a bit. Everyone was gone except us.

His dark eyes sparkled, playing with me. "Uh, is there a sentence in there somewhere?"

How to get the words out?

"I …" I gulped. How could I lose him? I just got him. I couldn't bear to lose him. I looked at my feet. "Thing is, you're so … and you would expect and quite right and I can't just yet what you expect and Kit said I should say so. I want to kill her, but then I agree, the truth and all, no games, no lies, and I don't blame you, 'cause I can't, not now." I watched him, watching me, tracking his reaction to whatever it was I'd said.

I take it all back! I screamed in my head. I braced for a pain that I knew there was no bracing for.

"Kit," he sighed, "is wise beyond her years. Are you saying you want me to be a *good boy*?"

I felt my eyes get prickly. What did I expect? Things like this don't.... He shook his head. *No, don't, don't, please....*

David took my hand and put it under his cotton shirt. His heart was racing. "I've waited two years for you, Sophie. I'll wait longer. I only want you." He pulled me closer. "It'll be okay. I'll take care of you, Sophie. I'll protect you." He sighed, took my hand back out from under his shirt, and kissed it. "Even if it's from me."

I fell into him and he held us.

It was like my soul finally came home, sat on the couch, and made itself comfortable. I knew in that moment three big things were true and I would remember them forever. One, I believed this boy. Two, I loved this boy. And three, maybe things like this *could* happen to people like me.

25

Papa picked me up after my shift at Mike's on Saturday, the last Saturday in February. It was time for his present. He waited for me in the Luigi limo and kissed me as soon as I got in. Then he made a big show of trying to look semi-stern. "So, Sophie, tell me, how is your young man?"

"Unbelievable, Papa. You just wouldn't believe it and even more unbelievable, my 'young man' is crazy about me! I think."

"How could that be anything but believable, Sophie?"

"Easy for you to say." I smiled. "You're blinded by the parental obligation of loving me. Speaking of which, where are we going and what's my present? I can't wait. What a week, what a birthday week it's been, Papa, the best week of my entire life! There's really something to this praying and lighting candles and religion stuff, you know?"

Papa didn't say anything as I was bouncing off the car walls, but he smiled when he turned the key. "I'm taking you to my AA meeting."

"Oh goody! I …" Whoa, I was about to say how much I love those meetings when for once, miracle of miracles, I shut my mouth in time. "I can't wait to see what it's like and how it's helped you. Thanks, Papa. Really great present." I turned around to the back seat as if I had somehow missed her. "You didn't invite Mama?"

He flinched. "She couldn't make it."

Mama couldn't make it? Papa's jaw set. In profile he didn't look as boyish as he did full on. In profile, Papa looked middle-aged. Maybe he looked like that full on too. I hadn't looked lately. Not really. I used to examine my father's handsome face for clues, search for traces of anything useful, despondency, frustration, joy, drinking, always the drinking. Make it? Mama would have crawled out of a hospital bed to "make it." I felt like I had been run over.

I had had seven miraculous days. Seven days of as close as I was ever going to get to being at the centre of it all in a world that made sense.

"Papa?"

We pulled up to a pretty little church near Auntie Eva's. He parked just down the block. It was a Unitarian church. Normally, I would've asked Papa what the heck a Unitarian was and whether I should add one to my altar. We would have done shtick. Not this time.

"What's happening, Papa?"

He took the key out of the ignition and crumpled.

So did I. *I take it back. Don't answer! I don't want to know! Don't …*

"Sophie, your Mama and me …"

He didn't have to say it. I didn't need to hear the words. I already knew. I knew for months. I knew when I saw them together, at the funeral, at Christmas, and even at my party. I also knew that, if the actual words hit the cold, steamy air, I wouldn't be able to pretend anymore.

"Sophie." He squeezed my hand. "There will never be anyone else for me but your Mama."

Could my mother continue without my father? Would the sun ever come out for her again?

"And you are everything to me. You were from the day you were born." He dropped his head. "You must know this, Sophie." Papa scrubbed his face with his hands. "But no, I can't. I won't be coming home."

I saw them clearly now in my head, what I had avoided seeing each time. They would stand together, closely even, but while Mama was totally there and shining for him, Papa was on guard, like he was marking his exit. "Ever?" I asked.

"I am stronger, but I am not strong, not yet, maybe never." I was about to pounce on that when Papa brought a finger to his lips. "It's true. And it's also true I'm tired of being a loser, Sophie. I have to be responsible for myself and take responsibility for my actions. I now know that I have to move forward, not back, if I'm going to get a chance at this sobriety thing. I've been a loser for the past twenty years, almost the entire time with your Mama." He lit a cigarette with the car lighter and blew smoke into the rear-view mirror. Into his own eyes.

Loser? Did he say loser? My father was the sun king.
Loser? Nothing was making any sense and still I was not
surprised. I think I knew from the moment he packed up his
little suitcase all those months ago. I never once asked him
when he was coming home. I knew.

But I had kept it a secret from myself.

"You can't blame Mama! That you feel like a loser, I mean.
It's not her fault."

Was it?

"Of course not, Sophie. I'm the weak one, only me. It's
entirely my weakness, not hers, but see, together somehow we,
I … and I'm still too shaky in this."

"But what about Mama?"

"I believe your Mama knows this and deep inside of her
she accepts."

Like hell, I thought. Sobriety had clearly impaired his
judgment.

"She must know even better than I do. Seven years in
prison, all the drinking before that, all the drinking after, the
blackouts, the shame, the guilt, so much guilt, Sophie, so
much guilt. Too much has, see sometimes what happens is
that, too much …" He slumped over the steering wheel.

"… has happened," I finished for him. I flashed to Luke
that last day in the park. "Too much has happened," I repeated.
"You can't find your way back." This, I understood.

He nodded. "What matters in this is you, Sophie. We both
love you so much."

"You love me more."

I might as well have slapped him. He turned away. "I'm

ashamed I let you think that. I love you *differently* because your Mama let me. She did all the hard work, the jobs, the moves, the scraping, the worrying, day after day with no help. Even before prison, Sophie, she did all the heavy lifting so that I got to come in with balloons and poems and magic mirrors for my princess."

I didn't say anything. We both knew it was true. We sat there for a bit while I tried to take it in. Just before I started to wallow, Papa jumped out of the car and ran over to open my door. He always had pretty fierce timing. "Will you do me the honour of accompanying me to my meeting?"

Dear Moses, Mama was going to be a train wreck. Worse. All right, well, I've seen that movie, and we got through it all the other times. *It'll be okay, it'll be okay, it'll be …* I inhaled slowly and exhaled slower still. "The honour is mine, Papa."

He took my arm and we walked into the meeting like we were walking the red carpet. I allowed the familiarity of it all, the warm feeling of the greetings, to wash over me.

"Welcome."

"How're you doing?"

"Glad you're here!"

"Welcome!"

Papa knew everyone and it was like I did too. That's what they do. *Welcome! You belong. You're safe here.* That was it! The feeling I had been chasing the whole year. It was the reason I loved that very first AA meeting. Wait, if I stopped being a drama queen for a minute, I had to admit that I felt safe with my Blondes, I felt safe with the Aunties, and I sure felt safe in David's arms. Mama and Papa? Not so much and not for years, if truth be told.

"Hi, my name is John and I'm an alcoholic."

"Hi John."

John outlined the evening's program, reminded us that we must respect the anonymity of every single person at the meeting and then led us into that prayer that I like so much.

"God grant me the serenity to accept the things I cannot change."

Papa caught me reciting along with everyone and raised an eyebrow.

I broke down instantly. Pathetic spy, I'd make. "Auntie Eva led us on a fact-finding mission back in September, and I've been a couple of times since," I blurted as we sat down.

Papa shook his head, but I could tell he was biting the inside of his cheek.

After some announcements, John made way for the guest speaker for the evening.

"Hi, my name is Kurt and I'm an alcoholic."

"Hi Kurt."

Kurt was a hippie, circa 1969. He looked like John Lennon, complete with long, wavy hair parted in the middle and granny glasses. Kurt told us that he was honoured to be telling his story at the request of tonight's celebrant, Slavko. Papa grabbed my hand and put it on his jangling knee.

"Papa?"

He nodded and I did the math. Sweet Jesus! It had been a year since me and the Blondes went tearing around the city looking for him, a year since his last bender, a year since he moved out. It had been a *year* since my father had had a drink. I squeezed his hand hard as much to stop myself from crying as to acknowledge his mind-blowing achievement.

Kurt had been sober for seven years, one day at a time. He was a Vietnam vet who came to Canada to escape his demons, only to find out that they had a passport too.

Kurt talked about damn near killing his brother-in-law over a hockey game and about living on the streets for five months. He talked about "getting it" in this room and how he was privileged to be connected to such amazing human beings, of whom one of the most amazing was Slavko. It had been a long time since Kurt had encountered such a trough of shame in one man countered by such a willingness to be open and receptive to help and to work the program.

"Slavko, please come up and receive your one-year medallion to mark twelve months of continuous sobriety."

Thunderous thumping and heartfelt applause carried Papa to the podium. Years melted away with every step, and by the time he got there, Papa was young again. He thanked his sponsor, Kurt, and everyone in the room. He also thanked God, which was pretty shocking, but even more shocking was that he went out of his way to thank Mama *and* Auntie Eva. Papa's greatest enemy had turned into his greatest friend.

"People cared for me, despite what I did or did not do for them," he said. "They cared when I least deserved it. They cared when I was the most ashamed and rightly so." He paused, to control himself. "And the one who cared the most is the one I hurt the most, my baby girl, Sophie." Papa extended his hand toward me. "I have so, so much to be thankful for, but I am the most thankful for you, my wonderful daughter. You, dear girl, are the reason I am standing here. God bless you, Sophia, happy birthday, baby girl, and thank you, thank you all."

Kurt gave him a back-smacking hug and then every single person in the room stood up for my father. Papa smiled back at us through tear-smeared eyes. Oh sweet Jesus, Buddha, and Moses, he was going to be okay. I have been watching and waiting on my father since I was seven years old. Even during all those years we didn't see each other when he was in prison, I carried him as best as any little girl could. And now he would be fine.

I could let go.

When Papa got back to our row, he hugged me so hard it hurt.

"Happy birthday, Sophie!"

"I love you Papa. This is the best birthday present of my life!"

The meeting wound down and Papa was swarmed. Everybody came by to shake his hand or slap him on the shoulder and offer a gruff "congrats, man."

We were pretty well the last ones out. "How about we get some milkshakes to celebrate? There is a 'surprise dinner' celebration at the Lobster Trap tonight at eight for all of us. But how about a milkshake with your old man now?"

"Will Mama be there?" I asked. "At the restaurant, tonight?"

"I hope so." He waved to a straggler. "But maybe not."

Reality pierced our celebration bubble. Mama. Somehow, she had managed to keep both of his big secrets from me.

Papa's one-year sobriety medallion and Papa not coming home. She gave me my week, a whole week of being in a miracle bubble. How much did it cost her? Would she have retreated to her room by now? I felt myself go small inside.

"I'm going to keep renting at Eva's," Papa said because he could always read my mind. "There's lots of different ways of being a family, Sophie."

The Blondes, the Aunties, he was right, I guess. Most families were messy, not just mine, not just me. I think I nodded.

Papa stood there waiting, looking like a hopeful twelve-year-old with his hands shoved in his pockets.

"If it's okay with you, Papa, maybe I'll pass on the milkshake part right now, but I'll definitely for sure be ready to celebrate like crazy at the restaurant with you and everybody tonight."

"And your …"

"And I'll try to get Mama to come." He looked relieved. "But no promises, okay? Right now, I think I want to go home." I let the word roll around in my mouth. I never called it that, never called any of our places that all these years. They were the apartment, the flat, the condo, not *home*. The word felt odd, sticky, like it would catch in my teeth.

"Home?"

"Yeah." I nodded. "I need a bit of time, Papa, and more importantly, I think Mama needs me. Actually, I think maybe Mama needs me to need her right now."

We walked toward the car. "And how may I ask, are you going to accomplish that?"

"It's time to paint my room!"

Papa laughed. "Genius!"

"Yeah, well, it really is time, and I know what I'm going to do. Remember my *Endless Summer* poster?" Papa nodded, but he didn't remember. That was okay.

"Anyway, it's in these beyond awesome shades of hot pink, psychedelic orange, and electric yellow. I'm going to paint each wall one of those colours and then hang the poster on the remaining white wall. It will make her demented, but she's the one who's been after me all these years to fix it up. Then there's the furniture and bedding …"

"I see endless weeks of operatic arguments over paint and fabric samples." Papa threw his arms around me. "I repeat … genius!"

"Yeah, and even if it's not the perfect plan, at least I'll finally have a finished bedroom. Hey, I deserve a decent bedroom!"

"You, Sophie Kandinsky, deserve a palace." He winked and then opened the car door for me. "So …"

"So, I want to go *home*, Papa." A little less odd this time, less sticky. I could get used to it.

He fired the ignition and the car purred into life.

"Okay, Sophie." Papa tried to smile, and then he tried harder.

"Home it is."

Acknowledgments

It takes a shocking amount of work by a shocking number of people to turn my words into a book. My husband, Ken, and my daughters, Sasha and Nikki, are not only first-class first readers but indefatigable cheerleaders as well. My writing group, the infamous GOUP, did a lot of heavy lifting. Thank you, Loris Lesynski, Ann Goldring, and especially Nancy Hartry and Susan Adach. Margaret Morin, Paula Wing, and Marie Campbell were indispensable—again. I am deeply grateful to the ever-patient and talented Penguin team, including Vimala Jeevanandam, Lisa Jager, Dawn Hunter, and Karen Alliston, and to Caitlin Drake, who made my Blondes better than they would have been without her. And finally, to all of *my* own Blondes and Aunties, who always were and still are my inspiration, *puno ti hvala*.